The Quintessence of Shadow

By J Andrew Evans

© Text: J Andrew Evans © Snaede endeavours 2021

The Quintessence of Shadow
A Crystals prequel   by J Andrew Evans
Part of the Singer Series   © Snaede endeavours
All Rights Reserved

Text Copyright   © J Andrew Evans, 2021.
This edition Copyright © Snaede Endeavours 2021.
ISBN: 9798530537103

The characters and situations in this book are entirely imaginary and bear no relation to any real person or actual happenings. All rights reserved. No part of this publication can be reproduced, stored in a retrieval system, or transmitted in any form or by any means, electronic, mechanical, photocopying, recording or otherwise, without the prior permission of the publishers and/or authors.

© Snaede Endeavours. Paperback Edition. 2021

◈ The Singer Series ◈
of
Fantasy novels

The Quickening of Water
The Awakening of Fire
The Transformation of Wind
Comprising the trilogy The Singer of Days

Crystals prequel
The Quintessence of Shadow

If you'd like to receive information about future books in the Singer Series, please sign up on our website:
https://snaedeendeavours.com

Look out for the next Crystals prequel in February 2022 entitled
◈ **The Clarity of Darkness.**

◈ **Followed by The Rhythm of Grass
Later in 2022**

It is planned that the series will continue with a galactic trilogy, a sequel to The Singer of Days.

J Andrew Evans, October 2021

Map of the world

If what you desire is not all that you are . . .
. . . then heed the call of what is.'

From the teachings of Swamp Mystic Blopez

Contents

CHAPTER 1	1
CHAPTER 2	14
CHAPTER 3	28
CHAPTER 4	40
CHAPTER 5	50
CHAPTER 6	61
CHAPTER 7	74
CHAPTER 8	86
CHAPTER 9	98
CHAPTER 10	106
CHAPTER 11	118
CHAPTER 12	128
CHAPTER 13	137
CHAPTER 14	149
CHAPTER 15	159
CHAPTER 16	168
CHAPTER 17	177
CHAPTER 18	185
EPILOGUE	193

A Crystals Prequel in the Singer Series

Chapter 1

*'Let the mystic hear and increase in learning;
the one who understands will find the path'*

Mystic Turlep

Parlòp did not like the floating city – but it didn't much like her either.

She heaved herself out of the water onto the entry-raft, then turned and called a summoning on Saimar. The allarg looked at her from the deep river and indicated his disapproval of the city with a low testy growl. He was not pleased. They had left the swamp. It was their place. Parlòp growled a sound in response, sending a voice to him. The allarg made his ungainly arrival onto the boards of the city. The surface dipped slightly under his weight, but it quickly righted, such was the weight of the guard buildings on the raft.

Parlòp turned and considered the sight before her. There were sentry huts, but no riverguards were visible. She looked through the gateway beyond the huts. The river people were staring at her from the city proper already. Their gaze was not friendly. She hated the way the men leered at her nakedness with a strange mixture of contempt and lechery. It just showed what brutes Kelsar men were.

The women were not much better. They looked at her angrily for making their men gape open-mouthed at the swamper seductress and remonstrated with the men next to them.

Parlòp pulled a shift from her wet-leather pack and pulled it over her head, hiding her body from their gaze. It was not perfect. She was soaking wet and the dress stuck to her form in unfortunate places. The men still leered. But such was the lot of the swamp people and this treatment was all they could expect in

Kel'Katoh.

If not for the order of her Grandee, she would not be here. She voiced to Saimar to keep close and released him from the summoning. Perhaps these Kelsar men would be more respectful of her with a loosened allarg walking beside her. Saimar let off a growl of joy at his freedom. She glared at him but the look in his eyes told her that he understood. He wasn't to eat anything she didn't allow – especially not any river people. The allarg waddled in an ungainly fashion towards the Kelsar who were gathering at the end of the raft walkway. They did not like that a swamper had dared to come. They looked at her with a mixture of fear and anger – this Solpsara woman, this shameless swamper walking towards them with a wild allarg beside her.

Saimar growled his defiance. He did not care and neither did she.

Quite a crowd of Kelsar had gathered to glare at her now. They divided to let her pass through the gates, curious. No doubt they hoped she would carry on into the city, away from them.

She stepped beyond the last of the crowd at the end of the entry walkway, an open area spreading out before her. The entry-raft was placed near the market square of the city. There were crowds of Kelsar there, trading, calling, shouting, and many stalls and booths on market rafts and barges, stretching out across the plaza. An even larger number of the flaxen-haired riverfolk gathered around the stalls of the market turned to glare at her and her allarg.

A man stepped before her – a riverguard. He looked intensely annoyed. Perhaps it was because she was from the swamp; perhaps because he should have been on guard at the sentry hut outside the gate and had been, instead, enjoying the market. Parlòp did not know or care.

'What is your business here, swamper?' He looked disgusted at the sight of the green-hued skin of a Solpsara. His lip was curled upwards as if he wanted, above all things, to cast the slime-woman from Kel'Katoh and back into the swamplands where she belonged.

Some of the more foolish riverfolk believed that the swampers had green skin – stupid as they were. Maybe he was one of them. He looked brainless enough. The sensible, even among the Kelsar, knew that the Solpsar stained their bodies with pastes made from the sap of the nargon tree. It gave good protection against the cold and was effective camouflage against the Kelsar – a truth they had learnt to their cost many times when they foolishly forayed unasked into the swamp. She understood his dislike of her. The Solpsar despised the flaxen-haired runnelers too. Swamp and river did not mix. All knew it.

She gazed at him impassively and stroked the muzzle of Saimar beside her with her bare foot and the allarg growled in appreciation. The Kelsara looked down at the beast with unease. Her point was made.

'I come at the command of my Grandee,' Parlòp said to end the aggressive silence between them. 'The Kelsari requested a mystic to come. The Solpsari, the excellent one, deigned to agree. My Grandee obeyed his commands. I am sent.'

The guard looked palpably unconvinced. 'What would the Kelsari want with a swamper and a scheming mystic such as you?'

'You must ask him that question, I suppose. I was not told – I was merely commanded to come. If you wish I shall return home and explain to my Grandee that you did not permit my entry. What is your name, Kelsara, that I can tell who it was that prevented my summons and the Solpsari, the excellent, can report back to your king that it was your fault?'

Anger flashed across his features. But, despite that, he looked a little less sure of his ground. The undisguised disgust on his face did not fade. He did not speak, he just glared at her, unsure.

Parlòp continued stroking the allarg's muzzle with her foot, crinkling her toes to rub his gnarly skin. 'Why not take me to someone with authority, Kelsara? Someone who can actually make the decision and obey your king.'

The guard looked, if possible, angrier at her presumption. She crouched down and ran a hand down the back of the allarg.

'The allarg cannot come,' he said.

'Tell him yourself, runneler. He goes where he wills. If you disagree with him, then deal with him yourself.'

Saimar growled aggressively, sensing the emotion between them. In a moment the allarg would strike, for an allarg attack was always the best defence.

Parlòp decided that this was going to end badly. She would let the allarg kill this guard and then, sensibly, she would hastily absent herself from the floating city. Returning to her temple, she would be able to tell her Grandee they would not admit her, and that, unfortunately, she had been unable to prevent her beast from killing a runneler guard.

Sad, but they would find another mystic easily enough – and she would have avoided these Kelsar once and for all. She tensed her muscles to flee once the Saimar's teeth closed on him.

'What is this, Casma?' Another guard had appeared from the floating stalls and was approaching, nimbly leaping from barge to raft.

Casma turned and looked a little unnerved. 'A swamper woman, Officer Krasne. Claims to have been summoned by the Kelsari. I was just about to expel her.'

Krasne arrived beside the riverguard. He looked her up and down, evaluating everything in a glance. 'Please, what's your name, Solpsara?'

Parlòp was amazed by the politeness of the request. She would be reasonable. She voiced calm to Saimar, and he snarled quietly in response. 'I am Parlòp, mystic of the Grandee Tarbap. The

Kelsari sent word through the excellent, the Solpsari Fleráp, that he wanted a swamp mystic to come. I was sent.' She paused. 'The allarg is Saimar.' The allarg beside her let out a long low growl as he heard his name.

Casma glanced down nervously.

Krasne shrugged. 'We have no orders about your coming, mystic. But come with me and we shall find the truth of your words. I will take you before the Dawen. He will know.'

Parlòp shrugged. She knew that Dawen was what the Kelsar called their Grand Vizier. Regrettably, this was heading in the direction of her having to fulfil her mission. She should have released the allarg sooner.

Now she would be bound by the order of her king to do whatever it was the riverking wanted. She felt a little irritated that she couldn't slip quietly away and report an aggressive expulsion from Kel'Katoh. She cursed her poor luck. But then another part of her wondered what the Kelsari could possibly need of a mystic.

Unhappily, she was about to find out.

Krasne led. Parlòp followed him, with Saimar waddling beside her. Casma took up a position at her rear. She did not like him, unseen, behind her. It did not feel safe. But she knew that Saimar would not permit an attack on her. She had been wise to bring him against the aggression of the Kelsar.

They hopped, jumped and walked their way across the floating market, attracting a lot of unfriendly stares. The Kelsar traders and shoppers were angry and affronted at her presence. She made her way without even bothering to return the glares.

They reached the edge of the market. The walkways were steadier, being part of larger houserafts. They weaved a tortuous way over narrow bridges and down alleys formed between the houserafts. Finally, they reached the largest of the barges, a great flat-bottomed boat, where the palace of the Kelsari was situated. The wherry was close to the rocky island around which the floating city was formed. On this island, protruding from the river like a broken bone, was the ruin. Vyderbo they called it. A word of an ancient language, its meaning long lost. It was a great monolith of a place, a memory of the ancient world that had somehow survived the eight hundred years since the ravaging.

She knew it was broken but it was still magnificent. Parlòp had never been so close. She had gazed at it from the river sometimes, curious what historical secrets it would reveal to her. She would have given much to study it. So she looked up at the craggy island with interest, but the height was too great for her to see anything of import.

Vyderbo was a memorial of the great magician kings for her, and it also represented the ruin of their world. It should have been open to all peoples – a monument to history. This ancient city was a place of the Malasar and their champions, the Left Hand and the Right. It should not have been the sole possession of the runnelers.

The Great Maven, the Left Hand himself, had taught her people how to speak to life. Their facility with animals was well known, even by the runnelers, but the reality was more than they could ever have understood. The ancients had taught them of control and communication – the Voice, the Summoning, the Understanding and the Order – not only of animals but of all forms of life. It formed the secret gift of the Solpsar. She did not find it so easy with other people though. They were too complex, too tricky.

They had reached the imposing palace, comprising two storeys. Whilst mostly formed of the wood the Kelsar used for construction, it had some finials and decorations in stone. It was grander than Parlòp had ever appreciated from the distance of the surrounding delta. She had looked on it a few times, safe in the Kelsar streams. She wondered at the desire of the Kelsari to cut and maim the wood to build their floating villages and city. It was so much more sensible to speak to the wood and allow it to shape itself.

But then, that was part of the secret.

There were two guards at the main entrance and Krasne spoke with them in the Kelsar tongue. Parlòp did not know enough of their language to follow what was said but the words 'She is expected' were definitely spoken by the taller of the two flaxen-haired guards.

Krasne turned to her. 'Please, Solpsara, the Dawen is within. He must speak with you before you may come before the king.'

A guard indicated the doorway with a wave of his hand and then cast a wary eye at Saimar standing beside her. The allarg cast an equally suspicious eye at the guard.

'Must the allarg come?'

She laughed gaily, enjoying their discomfort. 'He is with me. So he comes.' She peered across at him. 'You can ask him to leave if you want. His name is Saimar. He may do as he's told.'

The guard did not seem to share the joke and dismissed Krasne and Casma with a gesture. He turned on his heel and strode into the building, not looking back to see if she and the allarg followed. They entered a wide hallway and he quickly strode up the grand stairway. Parlòp regretted even more ever being persuaded to leave her swamp and the temple she had guided into being. She followed forlornly up the stairs, Saimar slithering beside her.

They entered a great audience chamber at the top of the stairs and the guard, now peremptory, told her to wait there without even turning to check she was there. He disappeared behind the throne at the far end and through a doorway in the rear wall.

Parlòp crouched down beside the allarg who looked distinctly uncomfortable with their surroundings and was swishing his tail from side to side. She rubbed his snout and scratched between his eyes. The tail stopped its incessant angry twitching and Parlòp let herself slip to the floor to sit cross-legged beside him.

'This is a bad idea, Saimar, isn't it?' She looked across at the allarg. 'We should be back in our swamp.'

Saimar growled a long low growl of annoyed agreement. This was no place for him and he knew it. But he stayed. She did not have him summoned anymore or even ordered. He stayed because he respected her. They had known each other for many years. He was hers and she was his. He knew her.

A short round flaxen-haired man in a long robe appeared through the doorway behind the throne. The guard and a third man followed. The last was a tall thin Kelsara with a strong, powerful look to him. His hair was darker than the norm. He exuded strength and purpose and, even when silent, he almost glowed with unseen power. Parlòp could have found this third man attractive. She liked strong men, but his strength was warped by something, unpleasantness probably. He was undeniably powerful, attractive and competent, but not in a good way.

The Dawen was the short round man in the robe. He had three daggers at his belt, which was overkill, she thought, for gutting fish – a major preoccupation of the runnelers. He hurried towards her. She, assiduously, did not rise to her feet but remained sitting on the floor beside Saimar. The Kelsara Dawen stopped several feet from her, eyeing the visibly unrestrained allarg beside her.

'I am Torgane, Dawen to the king, Solpsara. We appreciate the willingness of the Solpsari to send a mystic to us. We mightily appreciate your coming. We hope you can aid us in this matter.'

'What matter is that?' said Parlòp and, twirling, rose to her feet in a single sensuous motion – an ophid ready to strike. She saw the reaction in the men to the physicality of the movement. They disgusted her. All Kelsar men did. Saimar growled, sensing her distrust and distaste.

'The king wishes to tell you that,' said the Dawen hastily, wringing his hands in grief. He did not look like a dangerous man, despite the multiple knives. 'But it is the most important matter, most important. You must come before him now. We have been waiting impatiently for your offices. We need your skills. You are a mystic, yes?'

Parlòp nodded.

'And your purpose is to understand.'

Parlòp considered him. 'Yes, it is the function of a mystic within the people. To see, to understand and to teach.'

'That is what we need . . .'

Parlòp looked up at that. 'Do you not have your own wize? People of the thaumato? What need have you of the wisdom of my people?' She knew, even as she said it, that the wize of the Kelsar had very great disdain for the primitivism of the swamp people and believed, without question, in their own superiority in all matters of knowledge and understanding. What possible reason could they have to use a swamper mystic?

'It is a matter of trust, Solpsara,' said the unpleasant powerful man at the Dawen's side.

'This is Caresma,' the Dawen said. 'He is my adviser and Fount of the Wize order.'

Parlòp cautiously acknowledged the Fount. 'I am Parlòp, mystic to the Grandee Tarbap.'

'Then come, mystic Parlòp. I will conduct you to the king.'

He came forward as if to take Parlòp's arm.

Saimar let out a long warning growl and the Dawen stopped and scuttled back. He looked nervously at her and indicated that she should follow him.

◊◊◊

The king was not in the palace but in a boat on the river just behind the palace, bobbing beside the great rock of the Vyderbo towering above them. There were few barges here; walkways and bridges connected the palace with the paths up the rock. It gave the Kelsari a wide pool behind his palace in which he could indulge the Kelsar passion for fishing.

Parlòp would have loved to abandon them all and explore the

ruin above them – alone.

As they arrived, Saimar took the opportunity to plop noisily into the river beside this great skiff of the king. He did not go far but lay, just at the surface of the water, gazing at them, ready in a moment to leap to Parlòp's aid. She looked at him gratefully.

Sitting at the far end of the skiff, the king was indeed fishing. He was a tall man, fair as so many of the river people were. But his hair was almost white in its sun-bleached fairness. He was surrounded by courtiers, all Kelsar like himself. They were mostly relaxing and not filling their time doing anything useful.

A woman was there, dressed very differently in long pale blue robes. She was of a different complexion too, darker in hair than the Kelsar, her tresses the colour of sandy rocks and her eyes strong and piercing. She would be a match, Parlòp was sure, for the angry, fearsome Fount of the Kelsar wize, Caresma. She looked up as the party arrived and gave Parlòp a piercing and somewhat unfriendly stare. It was as if she wanted at that moment to penetrate beneath the simple shift and green-hued nakedness. She wanted to discern her utterly – and through that knowledge, control. For the first time in her whole unwelcome arrival in the floating city, Parlòp felt truly naked. This woman did not want to lust. She wanted to dissect.

The Dawen Torgane bowed low before the king and, Parlòp saw, Caresma did too, although much less obsequiously. Torgane spoke as soon as his head was up, without the king saying or doing anything.

'Wellspring of your people, may I present the mystic Parlòp, who has been sent by the Solpsari to aid us . . .'

The king waved a dismissive hand at his Dawen. 'Greetings, mystic Parlòp. I am Chrasm, the Kelsari of the people. The Solpsari has been good to send you to us. We have a problem we need to understand and we believe that understanding is always sought by the mystics of your people.'

Parlòp bowed her head briefly, not too much, and she hoped less in obeisance than in recognition. 'It is true,' she said. 'It is our function. To see, to understand and to share.' She paused, wondering for a moment if she had better say what she was thinking. But then, she had already questioned the Dawen on the thought. She decided. 'Yet it is confusing, lord, why you require this service from us, of me. You have your own wize. There is wisdom among you. Why not use your own people if there is a question to be answered?' She stole a glance at Caresma standing beside her. He was looking at her and bowed his head slightly, as if in acknowledgement of her reserve.

'Yes, we do,' said the king without even looking away from the line of his rod in the water, which bobbed interestingly. 'But this matter pertains to the death of Kalanomena, the Chief Envoy from the Karsar – the emissary of Turganamena himself. He is the most powerful of the wizard lands.'

The woman with piercing eyes looked up.

'Here is Taraganam who also came with Kalanomena from his tower. She requests... that we thoroughly and... impartially investigate this matter, before she reports back to her Lord Turganamena.'

The king sighed and looked away from his fishing. As he did the float bobbed fiercely. The fish had waited for his inattention before arriving. Parlòp quietly voiced it to ignore the bait.

'We wish above all things to solve this matter. The Karsar suspect our foul play so they will not permit... or do not favour an investigation by our wize. We, on the other hand, do not wish to allow the Karsar unfettered access to this matter in case this death is but an excuse to bring war down upon us again.'

Taraganam looked for a moment as if she was going to interrupt the king but thought better of it.

'So our Karsar friends and our wize must be aided by a disinterested third party. One who cares only to discover the truth and to share it – and cares not who it favours.'

Parlòp readily understood there was a real risk here of another war between Kelsar and Karsar, with all the unnecessary suffering and pain that would bring. And he was right too that the Solpsar did not care either way. If the Karsar and Kelsar murdered each other that left one less of either of them to trouble the Solpsar and trespass in their swamp.

'The king feels you will discover the truth of this death and judge the matter fairly,' said Taraganam, the woman with the rock-sandy hair and piercing eyes. 'We do not seek war with the Kelsar. But if they have killed our ambassador there must be restitution or . . .'

The Dawen, Torgane, spoke. 'We have not . . . We are as puzzled as you.'

The king waved a lazy hand. 'So neither the wize of the Karsar –' he indicated Caresma '– nor the messenger of the Karsar lords, Taraganam, may investigate this matter. We wish you to do so. To search, to discover the truth and to share it with us. This is the function of a mystic.'

He looked over at Parlòp who nodded, slowly, reluctantly. What slime-ball had the Solpsari landed her in?

'They will, of course, both accompany you so that it is seen, by them, that you are not placed under any undue influence by either party.' Saimar took this opportunity to add a long powerful growl, which made everyone on the boat look over at the allarg.

Parlòp smiled. Was Saimar saying that preventing anything undue was his role? But he could not have understood their talk and she had not voiced him. He just understood the emotions.

They all turned back to gaze at her standing there, the green-skinned savage in the shapeless shift covering her naked body, her wet-leather sack over her shoulder.

What mudslide have I landed in?

'What benefit is there in this to the Solpsar people, king of the river?' she said strongly. 'Why should we do this service for you or the Karsar lords? This is truly nothing to us – an envoy dead? Why is this important?'

Chrasm, the king, smiled. He had clearly been expecting the question. She felt his smugness even with the difficulties she had sensing people.

'Friendship between swamp and river is always a goal between our peoples. Your Solpsari knows this...' The smile became obsequiously sly.

That meant that she had to do it because her Solpsari had already agreed to it. She had known it. She had not liked it. She was placed here, sent by him. She could not fail to complete the task without being disobedient to her king. This angered her even more than the idea of doing anything to aid the river people.

'Peace between our peoples would be easily achieved if your people would respect the borders of the swamp,' she said testily. 'Stop forays into our lands. Stop your people floating their villages into our swamp to steal the fish.'

Chrasm smiled. 'Quite so, mystic Parlòp. And these are all things that can be achieved if we have your aid in this matter. We will be grateful to your king.'

Parlòp smiled a bitter smile. She was caught. Swamp vines had her. She had no choice but to discharge her duty in this place. She let out a long sour breath. She glanced over at Caresma and then Taraganam – the two wize. She did not relish investigating anything accompanied by either of them, let alone both. She was ambushed by the naivety of her king – be he the excellent one or not. None of the benefits to the swamp would be forthcoming. She knew it even if he did not. It would be more likely that one side or another in this matter would end up blaming her and through her the Solpsar. Whoever was to blame for this death would not forgive her for hunting it out. For it must, surely, be the politics of one side or another who had killed this man. They would not want that revealed, let alone shared with all. Yet that was her purpose. She was a mystic.

Saimar growled again, long, low and angry.

Chapter 2

*'There is a way that appears to be right,
but in the end, it leads to death.'*

The poem of the mystic way

'His body was found here,' Taraganam said. 'His back was burnt from a great fire, but it was only his back. It looked as if the conflagration must have been thrown or cast at him from behind.'

'And on his front, there were claw marks from some great beast,' Caresma added quickly. He glanced meaningfully at Saimar.

The allarg lay next to Parlòp. She ignored the jibe, typical of Kelsar. Everything bad was the fault of the swamp. She looked down at Saimar. Whether he was protecting her or standing close to be protected, Parlòp was not sure. She didn't trust them either.

They stood in the centre of the massive ruins of Vyderbo on top of the great outcrop. Despite their height, Parlòp could still see the edges of the floating city. The great clusters of rafts, boats, skiffs, wherries and walkways were impressive. But to stand in the centre of the extraordinary ruin she had so often gazed at should have been enough of a reward.

But it wasn't.

'So, where is the body?' Parlòp asked the question but she already knew the answer.

'It was cremated in line with the custom of my people,' said Taraganam.

Parlòp was unhappy. It made the task more difficult – not to see and inspect the body herself. An uncharacteristic look of regret passed over the Karsara wizard's features.

'We both examined him very carefully before that was done,' Caresma said hastily. He clearly did not want this situation to get worse. He was to represent the interests of the Kelsari and to preserve the peace. He did not want the Karsar to be further angered, not only by the death of their envoy but by some real or imagined obstructiveness from the Kelsar.

'It is eight days since he died,' said Taraganam. 'It has taken this long to send messengers to your Solpsari and for you to arrive. We could not leave him any longer. It would have been disrespectful.'

Parlòp nodded. That was reasonable. But she would still have liked to see the body for herself. For how could she answer the truth of his death without being able to see his remains?

'So what is your explanation? How did he die?'

Caresma raised an eyebrow. 'Being burnt from behind and clawed by some terrible beast cannot have helped.'

Taraganam looked very offended at this insensitivity. She did not speak but merely glared at the Fount.

Parlòp sighed and Saimar, sensing her emotion, also growled his disapproval. Caresma looked down at the beast but there was no fear in his gaze, only scorn. He did not fear the allarg at all, which was strange. They were powerful animals. And all people knew they were unalterably wild and ferocious. All folk feared them for they were not afraid to attack people. The runnelers understood that only the Solpsar could tame them. No thaumato of the wize would protect him against the bite of an allarg. So why the confidence? She found it curious. But this was not the mystery she had been sent to seek out and to understand.

Parlòp walked forward, away from them. Saimar waddled after her. They were in the central square of Vyderbo. A great archway stood in the middle – some sort of ancient megalith, possibly from an age even earlier than the ruined city itself. It was constructed of a strange white stone the like of which Parlòp had never seen. Another mystery that she was not there to solve.

'Do you see any fire here, Caresma? Or any beast save mine? How came he to die like this, here, amidst a ruin that is empty of all but rocks and trees?' She turned quickly and looked pointedly at him. 'Is there anything in Vyderbo that could cause this?'

Neither of them replied.

As the silence stretched out, Taraganam walked forward towards the arch, past Parlòp. She stood gazing through it, her back to them both. 'We do not even know why he came here. We had arrived as an embassy between the Kelsar and my Lord Turganamena. We arrived and were given rooms in the Kelsari's palace. We were formally greeted in the throne room and then agreed to begin our discussions and negotiations the following morning after we had recovered from our journey. The journey had been long, across Karsar lands and the southern Kelsar holdings, then an arduous trek over passes of the Wasra. We were tired. We all ate together – not a formal meal, but with the Kelsari and his court. Then servants escorted us to our rooms. To sleep, I thought. It was late.'

Taraganam looked strangely wistful as if she were pondering on some nostalgic thought that she did not share. 'The following morning I rose late. The servants had not woken me. I went to break my fast with him. When he did not appear I sent them to find him. He was not in his rooms. The bed had not been slept in. We searched the palace – and then the city. He was eventually found here.' She stopped and gazed solemnly at the ruins around them, steadfastly not looking at the spot where he had been found.

Parlòp followed her gaze. All the buildings, whatever they had been, were broken and smashed. Of them all, only the great megalith arch in the centre of the square was intact. Trees grew in the middle of many of the ruins – ancient trees long undisturbed. Parlòp knew that Vyderbo was a revered place for the Kelsar. She knew they would not rebuild here – for surely this rocky island would be a grand place to build strong buildings made of stone instead of the floating city around it – buildings of which the

Kelsari could be proud. Instead, there was this ancient ruin. It would only be rebuilt, the prophecies and myths had it, on the return of the magician kings. And few thought that day would come anytime soon. After all, it was eight hundred years since the almost mythical ravaging.

Parlòp gazed at the ruins and the ancient trees that grew amongst them. She would have liked to speak with the trees. They were not conscious, at least not in the way she was, or even Saimar. But they perceived. They knew sunshine and sustenance. They recognised danger. They would have an imprint, she knew they would, of what had happened, if only because it was fire that had killed him. Trees dreaded fire. Even in their vegetative state, it disturbed them.

'This is an ancient place, but it is a place of ruin,' said Taraganam. She moved her hand, indicating the ruined buildings around them. 'It is a monument, merely, a relic of an age long lost, never to return – despite the fables. There is nothing here but empty memories. Why come here? Someone must have been with him, met him here or followed him when he left the palace.'

'The king didn't even know he had left,' said Caresma stoutly. 'How could we follow him? And why would we kill him here, where the blame would fall on us?' He was keen to deny any culpability. 'The guards did not see him depart. They declare this. We swear it. He did not use the main doors. His trip here was clandestine and not of our doing.' Caresma was strident now. 'He must have wished his activities, whatever they were, to be secret – even from his own people.'

Taraganam looked irritated at that but she did not immediately speak.

Parlòp sighed and glanced again at the largest of the trees. What excuse could she find for going to that tree and by understanding find what dull perception the tree had of events around it? She must not reveal her true skills to these, Kelsar or Karsar. All the

Solpsar knew this. These warlike peoples would desire them beyond reason. What monstrous mayhem could they mete out to each other and the world if they gained power over life – but without the requisite respect? For they had already corrupted what small skills the thaumato gave to them into a thing of war and hatred.

'He could not have been killed by thaumato,' said Taraganam, strangely speaking to Parlòp's thoughts. 'He was too skilled to be fooled by a phantasm.' She glanced meaningfully at Caresma and then turned abruptly away from him as if dismissing the very idea that he was to blame.

'To produce fire from nothing is impossible.' She was now talking directly to Parlòp as if she needed an education in the wiles of the wize. 'It is easy to cast an apparition of fire. But it is not real – merely a trick of the mind. It could not have burnt him. And he would have known. A mighty clawed animal can be cast too, but it does not claw. The danger of thaumato lies in the minds of those who perceive it and fear it. Those who do not know what is real and what is false. There is no reality to the casting, only a distraction and the fear of not knowing. This fire must have been real.'

Parlòp thought she had rarely heard a more obvious point.

'Yet there is no sign of a fire having been here,' said Caresma. 'It was only on the body. Taraganam, you know this. We have discussed it many times before. And the fire from a handheld torch would not have been sufficient to burn him to that degree. Something unusual occurred – or it was not here that he died.'

'We did not recognise the claw marks,' Taraganam continued, ignoring Caresma and still staring directly at Parlòp. 'It was no beast that we know. Might your skills with animals help us to identify? The claws were large, whatever it was.'

Parlòp considered them silently. They had stopped sparring with each other and were now both looking at her as if she already had all the answers. Instead, all she had was a growing conviction that she would never resolve the matter – not to their satisfaction.

'We will see,' she said. 'We know nothing as yet, do we? He may have died here and the person or the thing that killed him has left, or been removed.' Taraganam looked as if she was going to speak. Parlòp ignored her and continued talking. 'Or he may have been killed, as Caresma just said, and brought here from wherever the death took place.'

Caresma said, 'To move a badly scorched body would surely attract more attention than him secretly getting out of the palace and coming here alone. There were no reports of either – of anything.'

'I do not know this place,' said Parlòp. 'Let me walk it and get some feeling for the ruin.' She hoped that this innocent-sounding excuse would give her time to understand with the trees, without the others realising what she was doing, why or how.

'I can show you round,' said Caresma and smiled his peculiar, powerful, scornful smile.

'I'd rather explore it alone,' said Parlòp hastily. 'And think . . .'

She walked quickly away from the two wize, the matter settled. They would not care. They would continue to spar with each other and get very little done. Typical of Karsar and Kelsar to always seek to blame each other and never to resolve anything. How many wars had they fought just for such bravado? Better to kill and die than ever admit you might be wrong. Parlòp looked around for the allarg. Saimar was basking in the sunlight near the archway so Parlòp left him to his tranquillity. He felt no danger in this place.

She wasn't sure that she agreed. But it was not a danger that any beast would sense. It was a danger born of politics.

She walked into the largest of the ruins next to the square. The tallest and mightiest of the trees was growing in the middle. The ruin had been a large and imposing building in its time, the walls high; the roof would have been far above her. She imagined fancifully that it might have been a temple to the Snake god or some palace. She idled her way to the tree, trying to look as if she wasn't going anywhere in particular. She glanced back at the two figures. They weren't looking at her but at each other. At that moment Taraganam clearly said something and Caresma quickly argued back. In moments they were deep into another tetchy quarrel.

Parlòp reached the tree and leant against it as if using it as a prop while she gazed around her. She touched the bark and called the understanding into being between them.

The tree was very old. Ancient beyond her comprehension, strong and vigorous. It had been safe here for a long time. It was not concerned much by what happened around it. It was complacent, deeply so. It was secure. It did not brood about the environment. It sensed it and did not fuss. It was content to just be. It felt little danger in this place.

There had been fire. Far away from it, over by the arch. It had been brief. It had not moved or come towards the tree. There was a flash, a stream of heat, and then it was gone. The tree cared no more. It was safe. It had returned to its serenity.

It was a good tree.

Parlòp looked over at the archway where Saimar was lying, still basking in the sunshine. *The megalith must be important.* Why had fire burst into existence by it? She walked slowly towards it. Saimar opened his eyes to gaze at her as she approached him.

The two wize saw her moving. They lost interest in their bad-tempered conversation and walked to intersect with her at the arch.

Parlòp reached it first and put out her hand to touch the smooth pale surface. She did not recognise the pure white stone, but she had not travelled far in the world. Her swamp was enough for her. Perhaps it was from the mountains to the west or those far across the plain in their north-west. They were the lands of the Hardsar and the Torasar peoples. She knew that. But all else was a mystery to her, one she had no intention of exploring further. She needed nothing they could provide.

The archway was intact. She thought again how strange that was – in the middle of such ruins as Vyderbo. No other structure she could see was complete. She rubbed the featureless surface and wondered. But there was nothing to be learnt here. Her powers did not extend to stone. It did not live. It was not.

The two wize arrived.

'Have you an idea?' said Taraganam.

'I was only thinking that it is strange that this arch survived when everything else that was Vyderbo has been ruined. And it was just beyond this archway that he was found.'

'It's like a gateway,' said Caresma.

They both turned to gaze at him. Parlòp wondered where that thought had come from. Did he know something?

He immediately looked uncertain. 'Like an arch in the middle of the main square that was the entrance to nothing and came from nowhere. A doorway to nothing,' he continued hurriedly. Slightly too quickly, Parlòp thought. It was almost as if he was testing them. Trying to ascertain if they knew something that he already did. Deciding how much they knew and then quickly dissembling when it revealed too much. Did the Fount know something about the arch that he was not sharing?

'Perhaps there was a building once,' said Taraganam, not picking up on the nuances of Caresma's statement at all.

Caresma interrupted her, perhaps grateful for the distraction. 'There is no sign of that.' He was shrugging now as if it was of no importance. Yet somehow Parlòp knew that it was indeed important. What was this mystery? Just another thing she was not here to solve, perhaps. 'Yet, you are right, it could have been.

Perhaps the stone of the building was valuable—'

Parlòp decided they were going to start bickering again. She bent down and greeted the allarg beside them with a friendly rub.

After tending to the allarg and assuring him of her care, she looked up. Taraganam was indeed arguing with Caresma. She did not bother listening to what they said. River and tower were so ridiculous. Their incessant wars were ridiculous. She would be happy the very moment she could leave and return to her temple.

'There must be a reason he came here,' she said, cutting across the Karsara in mid-sentence. Taraganam did not look happy.

'It is a ruin, a dead place,' said Caresma.

'There must be something. Let us assume he was not brought here dead. The Kelsar riverguards would surely have seen that. A single man might stealthily depart the palace but, as you said, people carrying a badly burnt body would not do so without someone seeing or hearing.'

'Of course,' said Caresma, pleased his defence was established.

'He must have been seeking something. He knew a secret of this place that we do not know. It could be anything. A small artefact buried here, a clue in one of the ruined buildings. The purpose of this arch. Do you know the ruin well?' She looked at Caresma.

'As well as any. I have lived in the city since I joined the wize order.'

'Doors? Things long buried? Is there any disturbance to the ruin? A sign that he, or another, was digging here, or trying to break through to something?'

'None that I have seen. There was a search but mostly in the immediate area – here, where he was found. We did not search every part of the place. It is a ruin. It's always been a ruin, of interest only to history and myth. We assumed that the key to finding his killer was working out what or who killed him here – nothing else. There is no reason to come here for its own sake. We thought he came here to meet someone, so their meeting was secret.'

'Is there more than merely these ruins of buildings above the ground? Is there something else – a hole, a basement, a dungeon? A way down inside the rock.'

'Well, there is the crypt.'

They both turned to look at Caresma.

'The crypt?' said Taraganam tersely.

'There is nothing there. We aren't even sure it is a crypt. We think of it as that because there might have been some tombs. There are some broken statues and carvings. Nothing else. No secrets. People have known of it for many centuries. Anything of value is long removed. It is just one room below the ground. It goes nowhere.'

Parlòp rose lithely to her feet, her hands leaving the gnarled skin of the allarg. 'Where is it?'

Caresma looked puzzled and bored at the same time. 'It is far off, over to the east of Vyderbo, in the last of the ruins before this rock drops back into the river. There is nothing. It is empty of all but memories – of things that are long forgotten.'

Taraganam was annoyed. 'You have not mentioned this before.'

'It is naught, that's why. A strange underground tomb, a cellar even, that has long been empty and is simply the haunt of disobedient children or a refuge for wild animals. There is nothing there.'

'Was it investigated when they found him?' Taraganam said. From her tone, she was ready to begin another bad-tempered argument with Caresma.

'It was ... is far away from where we found him. But what reason did we have really? Do we have one now?'

Parlòp moved. 'Show me,' she said. Saimar looked up from the ground and shambled after her. The two wize trailed after him. Caresma looked annoyed by the request and Taraganam peeved at him for not telling her before.

◊◊◊

They walked a good distance from where Kalanomena they had been found. The way to the vault took them past many ruined buildings and through broken streets.

But, Parlòp thought, it was possible that he was pursued all that way and simply caught by whatever had clawed and burnt him in the square. Not that she saw any indication of pursuit. If this ruin had been in the swamp or any place of living things, Parlòp would have known how to track, but in this wasteland of rock and stone, she could not fathom the signs. There were some trees and stubby bushes in the ruins, but they would have sensed nothing more.

Parlòp realised that Vyderbo was bigger than she had understood. It had been close to being a city on top of this rock in the middle of the widening river. Perhaps it was not surprising that the Kelsar had not searched everywhere when the envoy died. It was too great a task. Vyderbo was enormous.

As she walked she mused that it was indeed deeply surprising that the riverfolk had not built up here instead of anchoring their floating city all around it. Nothing but some abiding respect for the ancient nature of the place would explain why they had preserved it as it was, a ruined, broken place for eight hundred years.

The final building before the edge of the cliff was almost intact. The roof had collapsed but most of the high walls were there. Parlòp could see where the floors had been fixed on the walls inside. It was hard to credit but, incredulous, she realised the place had been four storeys high. The very thought of such skill in architecture was staggering. There were piles of broken stone littering the ground. Surely the upper floors had not been constructed of stone? How had the weight been supported? Were the walls that strong? She wandered into it, stunned by the stupendous achievement. It would take many mighty trees guided and grown for centuries to come even close to the size of this marvel in stone.

In the centre of the building, steps led down, underground. There had been stone balusters around them once, but they had been smashed when several large stones had fallen from above. Fortunately, the falling rocks had not blocked the way underground.

Parlòp doubted it was a crypt. It was surely a dungeon or a cellar.

Reaching the top of the steps, she gazed down. Some smaller rocks littered the steps but the way was still clear. She turned to Saimar and by voice told him she needed him to come with her. She knew she must insist. He did not like stairs. They were not natural.

They threaded their way down, wending their way past the largest rocks and splintered steps. Saimar slithered and skidded after them. It was dark at the bottom and Parlòp could not see properly in the dimness. Some sort of carved frieze ran along a long wall to her right. There might once have been a statue standing halfway down the opposite wall. Beyond it was what looked like a tomb, a great rectangular shape with the shaded form of a person carved into the top. She could not see the further end of the crypt. It was too dark.

She heard the rasping sound of a tinderbox being struck and turned. Caresma was trying to get a short torch alight. Wize as they were, they could not cast light, merely the phantasm of light, an image of something placed in the mind of their target. Not the reality, it did not light the world; it merely projected what the thaumatic wize wanted them to see. That was the only skill of thaumaturge – an image. To make people see something that was not there.

They could construct a whole world around someone, but it did not alter reality. Despite that knowledge, though, it was difficult to act in a reality that one no longer perceived.

But that was not the real threat of the thaumato, not as Karsar and Kelsar had corrupted it. The real threat was when they added something to reality, something that you could not decide was real or not. An army that was not there, but might be, an assassin that could not kill you – unless he did. An assassin you could not see, a building that did not exist, a bridge that was no escape. They had all led people to their real and actual deaths. Wars between river and tower were often won by the one who could trick the senses of the other best. It sickened her. It was merely the form of a thing and not reality. For her only the real was important. She was a mystic. Reality was her goal. To seek, to understand and to teach.

Caresma had the torch alight at last. It was a small one, easily held in his robes. It would not last long. They, none of them, had planned to descend into darkness.

Parlòp gazed out across the reality revealed. The crypt was a long low room. The long frieze along the right-hand wall was carved and depicted some great battle of long ago. It could have been one of the battles when the makkuz, the monsters from the stars, had come and ravaged the world. But no, it could not be, for that was when Vyderbo itself had been destroyed. Who would carve a frieze in a ruined crypt in a broken city? She now saw that the head and face of the smashed statue had been splintered by some great blow. She could not tell who it was meant to be.

At the far end of the room, was another bas-relief of a great pastoral scene. It was quite beautifully made.

Parlòp sighed. There was nothing here.

This was a dead end.

'That is odd,' said Caresma.

They both turned to look at him and Saimar growled from the stairs behind them. He was only halfway down. He had stopped as soon as he could see the bottom. Steps were not built for allargs. He had gone no further than he had to.

Caresma raised the torch and, with it, indicated down the room. 'When I was last here, that carving, the bas-relief on the far wall, was damaged at that side. A small thing, a few stones broken off – but now it isn't. Why would anyone repair it?'

Taraganam walked forwards abruptly. 'Could it be . . ?' She hesitated. 'Could it be an eidetic? Hiding something. They are very hard to cast but Kalanomena was a high master of them.'

Parlòp knew what she meant. An eidetic was a phantasm that remained after the wize who cast it had departed. It was fixed somehow in its place, in the minds of any that approached. It hid something, deceiving the minds of those who came. It was no more real than any other thaumatic illusion, but it was very much more dangerous. One did not suspect its presence because there was no wize there to cast it. It made you inattentive.

They walked forward. As they reached the end of the room Taraganam impulsively reached out to touch the wall. Her hand went through it. There was something else, something real, beyond what appeared to be the wall. She pulled her hand back, frightened at last of what reality might be waiting for them beyond the illusion.

'We have discovered where he came,' said Caresma glibly, and the torch in his hand spluttered and died. Saimar growled far behind them in the darkness.

Chapter 3

'He breathed the winds of existence;
and of being, came life.'

Tracts of Blopez

It was quite crowded in the crypt.

They had reported back to the Kelsari. Caresma had been insistent that they needed to update him on the discovery. The phantasm was hiding something. What, they did not know. But the Kelsari needed to know what they had found and be involved in deciding what happened next. None of them relished just stepping through it without knowing what lay behind. They had to be cautious. There might be a great chasm beyond the eidetic casting. Or beyond might be whoever or whatever had killed Kalanomena – waiting to strike.

And Parlòp thought, they needed proper torches.

The discussion before they returned was long. The solution preferred by everyone, the riverking, the Dawen and most of the court and the two thaumaturgists, Caresma and Taraganam, was for the two wize to attempt to remove the eidetic phantasm. Everyone had an opinion as to how that might be done, for it was not an easy task to break another's thaumatic casting. It had made for some highly tiresome arguing and very little action. Parlòp had been frustrated. She had stood, silently, watching their unnecessary wrangling. Everyone had an opinion.

But to her relief, after much fruitless verbiage, at last they had returned to the crypt. And now it was crowded.

The Kelsari had sent four guards armed with swords. He had insisted. They came not only to hold large torches for them to see but, it was hoped, to protect them against whatever horrors might lay within the eidetic. *It must be the monstrosity that killed*

Kalanomena.

In charge of the four was the officer, Krasne, who had brought her to the palace. He, she felt, might be sensible. The others were Barces, Tarsh and Wasama. Parlòp was introduced but she didn't really want to know.

Back in the crypt, she stood at the back. She crouched down to the right of the stairs, her hands stretched out over the allarg's back, rubbing the softer parts of his gnarly skin. Saimar was growling his approval. Everyone was ignoring her, which was very much what she preferred. They believed that they were about to find out what had led to the ambassador's death and her role was therefore completed. She was not so sure it would be that simple. Whatever was behind the eidetic image, it could not be that easy. Nothing ever was.

If it was, they had wasted her time.

She gazed at their backs. There would now be further delay as Taraganam and Caresma busily tried to break the eidetic. The riverguards surrounded them and most of them did not look like they wanted to be there. The two wize were gesturing and calling out but the phantasm did not fade or change. Parlòp sighed and rubbed the allarg's back harder.

'This is a masterful eidetic,' said Taraganam at last. 'Kalanomena was greater than I ever knew, to make such an image. It has an amazing span.'

Caresma did not look as impressed by the mastery of the dead Karsar envoy. He looked peeved, offended almost. He kept opening his mouth to speak and then closing it again; Parlòp wondered if they were going to start bickering once more. But the Fount seemed to think better of it.

'Shall we send a guard to simply walk through?' he said eventually. The guard next to him took a quick step back. His torch flickered in the breeze and created ripples of light around the crypt walls. Krasne turned and glared at him.

'Be still, Barces.' The guard did not walk back but stared at them gloomily.

Krasne turned back to the eidetic and the two wize. But Parlòp noticed he didn't volunteer to go himself either.

'Or the beast, maybe?' said Taraganam. Everyone turned and looked at Parlòp and Saimar crouched by the stairs.

She shook her head slowly and firmly from side to side and rose lithely to her feet. Standing, she spoke directly to Taraganam. 'No, he will not. He is entitled to live the same as all of us – all of you. He is not more expendable, wize Karsara though you be.' She considered adding that the wize woman should throw herself through but resisted.

Taraganam shrugged. She knew, as they all did, that if Parlòp refused, none of them could coerce the allarg. It would not happen. Taraganam turned back to the phantasm and, holding her head to the side, tried by whatever skill of thaumato once more to break the enduring image. Nothing changed.

Parlòp muttered a swear word. She strode forward. Saimar slithered after her. 'Give me a torch.'

She knew that the sooner this farce was completed the sooner she could return to the swamp. She could stand their delay no longer. They all turned and glared at her.

'But we do not know . . .' Caresma began.

'Then we shall find out.' Parlòp gave a sharp order to the allarg to remain and strode forward, seizing the nearest torch from Barces. She reached the false image and without a backward glance stepped through what looked like a solid wall. The light from her burning brand spilt into the area beyond. There was no great precipice or abyss beyond as they had all feared but simply, a few scant feet ahead, the real wall of the crypt, a large hole smashed into it. Tools lay around, which were obviously those that had been used to break it down. He had smashed his way through the carved relief as if it was of no matter and no worth.

And it had been quite beautiful.

Beside her, Saimar's head and the first part of his body appeared through the thaumatic wall. He growled ferocious dissatisfaction with her actions. She glanced back at the apparent half of an allarg stuck in a wall behind her and growled her disapproval. He had disobeyed her order.

He did not look sorry.

Parlòp turned back to the cavity. It was blackened around its edges as if some great fire had burnt it. But surely the fire had come later. It was not how the hole was made. Otherwise, why were tools scattered around that had been used to break through the wall? If you could burn your way through you would do just that. So, something had come later and burnt it. The same fire that had burned the back of the fleeing Karsara emissary? Had Kalanomena been pursued back through the hole and out through the eidetic by something casting flames at him?

But what hurled flame?

There were the dragons of the creation myth. They could shoot flames, but they were pure myth. No one believed that. Then the makkuz, who had ravaged the world, were said to be creatures of light and heat – although they could appear as people when they willed it. Was there a makkuz in there?

Parlòp was still musing on this when Taraganam appeared beside the allarg.

'You did not perish,' she said.

'No. I did not.' But then that was obvious.

Parlòp stepped forward and thrust the burning torch into the hole. There was a passage with steps heading down. So there had been a hidden entrance. A door that Kalanomena had known was there but did not know how to open, so he had smashed his way through.

Bending forward, in the light of the torch, Parlòp saw a landing at the bottom of the steps at the faintest end of the light. She was sure, even in the dimness, it was not a floor but a landing. More stairs went further down, both to the left and the right. It was quite a few yards below. They would have to descend to find out more.

She turned and looked at the allarg, still poised, half of him sticking out of the eidetic wall. 'Stairs, Saimar,' she said. 'Your favourite.' The allarg did not understand. She had not used the voice. But he growled general dissatisfaction with their situation.

Caresma and two riverguards, Krasne and Barces, stepped into view. It was becoming crowded between the phantasm and the real wall with the burnt and broken doorway. If anyone else walked through the eidetic image, one of them would be forced to descend the stairs.

Krasne took in the situation with a quick, decisive glance. 'Are we descending?'

Parlòp looked at him with renewed respect. 'There is little point in coming here if we do not. We are here to discover why the ambassador dug his way into this wall. And then why he met his end.' She glanced at Caresma. 'Note the burnt edge of the hole. After he had smashed his way through something burnt it. I surmise he was pursued out again by some great enemy shooting flames – out through the ruins and back to the arch before it caught him.'

'So we are seeking a huge clawed fiery monster?' said Taraganam scornfully. *She doesn't believe in the creation dragons either.*

'Leave the other two guards at the top of these stairs,' said Caresma sharply to Krasne. He thought he was, as the senior Kelsara, in charge. Krasne nodded in obedience.

Parlòp did not care. They were all needlessly concerned with their perceived statuses. Nobody just was. It was tiresome.

She turned and looked across at Taraganam. The wize woman was standing close to her. Parlòp saw something strange in her eyes. It was not just the flickering light of the torches reflected in their fierce blackness. There was a steeliness, an excitement in her. She gazed at the way through the wall with a strange hunger.

Had she understood something? Something she now knew and they didn't.

Parlòp had the same feeling that she had when Caresma called the megalith in the square a gateway. He had known something then that he did not share. Now Taraganam knew more than she was telling them.

But, if she had known why Kalanomena had come here, why would she have waited to follow him? She could have quickly followed him alone, readier than he was to meet an enemy. Or had she just now worked something out? What was the extent of her knowledge?

She was silent – so she wasn't going to share.

Parlòp had the sinking feeling that everyone knew more about this affair than she did. They all had some sort of aim, a purpose here that they were not sharing. All their knowledge was partial, she decided. If not they would have acted long before this. They needed to understand other things. Only then would they reveal their true objective.

Only she had the aim to understand the whole and reveal it.

She was a mystic. It was why she was.

This was not going to end well. She felt it in her bones. But to walk away did not seem to be an option. Her king, the Solpsari, the excellent one, had been outmanoeuvred by involving her at all. She was trapped. She had to see this through to some sort of conclusion.

She stepped through the hole in the wall and took the first step down the stairs. They all looked at her in surprise. 'Let's get on with it,' she said.

Saimar waddled quickly past them all to run after her. She walked down the stairs and she heard Caresma, Taraganam,

Barces and Krasne following the allarg. They made a lot of noise doing it and Parlòp decided that if there was a makkuz or a creation dragon down here it was getting a lot of warning.

She reached the first landing and turned to glare at them.

'Some silence is in order here,' she said tetchily. 'We do not know what we face.'

The two wize scowled at her. They were not used to a swamp woman taking charge – her skin painted green, dressed plainly in a simple, crudely made shift and naked beneath it all. She was a primitive, a lesser person.

Yet a mystic had, very often, to take charge, to be strong. It was her role to guide the people with the facts and to speak the truth to grandee and king. If not a mystic, then who?

From the first landing, two sets of stairs ran downwards, one to the left and another to the right. She raised her torch and peered down each of them in turn. Saimar was beside her, looking uncomfortable. This was not an allarg's place.

The rest of the party was still behind her, on the stairs. She saw nothing on the landing but the steps running down into the darkness. There was no way to work out which way the Karsara envoy had descended. She knelt to examine the floor more closely and then lay prone on the top step of each side to peer down into the darkness. On the left side, far below, at the edge of shadow, lay a broken piece of rock blackened by fire.

This was it. If the fire had blasted at him as he ran then, missing him, it burnt the wall.

'This way, I think,' she said and rising to her feet stepped down the first stair.

The Kelsar did not respond but Parlòp heard a quickly quashed gasp of excitement from the throat of Taraganam. She had some inkling of what was down here, Parlòp was sure.

There was more here than some errant Karsara envoy named Kalanomena wandering off on an errand of his devising. Surely he had got out of the palace with someone's help. He had come here for a reason – Taraganam now knew or suspected.

But how could Parlòp force her to tell them?

The steps went downwards. She passed another landing and saw a further one, below. She continued to descend. Landing after landing came and went and Parlòp thought they must now be deep within the solid rock of Vyderbo itself. The way led down into some vaults hidden in its depths. Still, they had not reached whatever their destination was. There were small rooms off the landings but they were always empty and lacking doors. They were merely resting places or storerooms that had long been emptied. She explored them carefully and then continued down.

No one else took over. They let her lead.

She was dispensable, after all.

As she descended she conjectured that there had been a time when the Kelsar had known of this place. Known that the wall at the end of the crypt was a hidden doorway. There must have been a way to open it – which Kalanomena had ignored and smashed his way through. Why had this place been walled off? Did they want to prevent careless visitors? Or something else? She needed answers to these questions. Otherwise, she had no idea what they were walking into.

She sensed something.

She stopped abruptly and Saimar beside her growled a low, suspicious growl. He sensed it too. He knew there was something below, something just beyond the next flight of stairs.

A beast—

But it was like nothing she had ever sensed before. It was strange and no beast of her world. Parlòp had not met, nor even recognised by her magic all the beasts in the world. But she knew their feel. They moved to the same rhythm – the hakkat and the kinfar of the plains, the hacsar and ponics of the mountain bandits, the jaksar and tigon of the forests. She had not encountered them all – of course she hadn't. But whatever it was, this was different. It was in a different key. It was sung with different notes – a discordant sound from some divergent music.

Krasne spoke. 'What is it?' Strangely, both the wize were silent. Had they, in whatever way the thaumatic magic worked, sensed something too? If so, they were not sharing. But then, neither was she.

'There is something ahead,' she said, but it was dangerous to reveal that she could feel every beast around her at all times. She felt their animalism, their emotions and their worries. That was the hidden magic of her people.

She must dissemble and pretend it was but a feeling, a hunch. The nameless knowledge that all people had when there was something unseen, hidden. Something they could not see but knew was there.

'What . . . do you think it is?' said Krasne.

'A living thing,' she said, worrying whether the phrase was innocuous enough. 'A person, a beast, there is someone ahead.'

'The claws . . .' said Caresma. 'It may be the beast that killed him.'

Parlòp ignored them and let her senses flow out to the creature. She needed the understanding to come so that she knew more than the simple, nameless presence that the creature was at the moment. She was aware that the others, as usual, went on talking, albeit in whispers. She crouched down and rested her hand on Saimar's head, let him feel what she felt of the creature. He too must understand or he would attack any mysterious other that came their way. It was his nature.

The beast ahead was bizarre and unfamiliar. But it was frightened. It felt as if the beast was constructed of terror and dread. As if someone or some event had twisted its psyche into constant horror. Parlòp let her sense move out to it and through gentle use of the voice tried to communicate, to let it know her presence, her desire not to harm or destroy.

She found nothing but fear and panic. They flowed back at her, filling her mind with panic. This beast was lost, lost in hysteria and darkness. She felt sorry for it then. It did not know where it was. It did not know what it was. It was nameless dread incarnate – and it did not know why.

She would have to touch it. There would have to be physical contact if she was to use the order to calm the animal's psyche. It was lost, it was hurt, although not physically, she thought. It was hurt mentally, a broken and splintered thing.

What could have happened to hurt this beast so much?

Saimar growled beside her and raised his snout. The beast was scaring him. A nervous allarg would surely strike. She let her calmness flood into his emotional core and his growl became a wary thing and not an agitated one.

'I will go down,' she said, rising to her feet and cutting across whatever the others were talking about.

They stopped talking at once and looked at her. She gazed back at them. They had been discussing how to approach the next step and perhaps, she did not know, were considering bringing extra forces to bear. That would frighten the creature further and likely result in conflict. A cornered beast would always attack.

'Alone,' she said firmly.

'I'll come with you.'

She was surprised. It was Krasne, the officer of the riverguard.

'I don't need you.'

'I can hold another torch.' He smiled and she realised that he had a grudging respect for her. Was this a Kelsara who actually had esteem for the swamp people?

Saimar growled. It was probably not what it seemed – that the allarg was lending his approval to the idea. But it sounded like it.

'The rest of you . . . stay here. And try not to argue too loudly.'

Parlòp turned away from them and walked quickly down the

steps. She did not look back but she could tell Krasne was following her. The light from his torch came behind her. Apart from that, he was silent. Perhaps here was a Kelsara that a swamp mystic could respect as well. Saimar scuttled down, uncomfortably, beside her.

She slowed as she saw the final landing beneath her. The creature was closer and, she thought, it sensed that she and the allarg were coming towards it. Before that, she had been but a nameless sense, an emotion, a general calm presence telling it not to fear. Now it knew she was coming. It panicked this beast that was constructed of fear.

She slowed and she voiced to it again that she, that they, were not a threat. They were coming to help, coming to give, coming to be peaceful. She felt the response in the creature, but the fear did not ebb. But it settled, like unctuous mud into a pool of slime.

The last landing opened out into a hallway that stretched off into the darkness. The beast was further on. She walked slowly forward. She sent an order to Saimar to keep back and waved back imperiously with her hand for Krasne to do the same. She had no weapon and she tried not even to think about weapons in case the animal sensed it. She never carried one. That was why she brought the allarg.

The corridor was wide and there were doors on either side. They were old and dusty and no one had even touched them for an age. Whatever was within them, Kalanomena had not investigated. That implied that when he made his way down to this place he had known exactly where he was going. It meant that there was no impulsive grasp of a moment's opportunity, no exploration of a place unknown. This was not a master of the Karsara wize finding something by accident and taking a chance. He had planned this. He knew where he was headed and, perhaps, what he sought.

She wondered if he had known of the beast. For surely it was not for this creature formed of dread that he had come.

A metal gate stood ahead, wide open. Beyond it was some great hall – of what import she could not tell in the light of their torches.

As she looked a shadow filled the gateway. It was darkness itself, blacker than the blackest of nights. In the swamp, even when the twin moons were set, the stars still gave light. This creature had none. It was made of shadow and night. And it was as lost – an abandoned traveller in a poisoned desert.

There were claws too, many claws, and many legs. It could hardly walk for the length of the talons on great paws. It was an impractical thing. It could not be a true beast. Its head was a great crested thing of spikes and prongs but Parlòp saw a great maw of a mouth, all teeth and fangs, and yet somehow no means to swallow. This thing did not seem to have the means to go beyond the destroying of its prey. It could kill but not devour. It was an impossible animal that could not eat and therefore could not be. Standing and gazing at it, Parlòp felt it had the form of a child's drawing of terror. A dark and twisted thing that filled the nightmares of a child – but would never really live.

And if once you reached its grasp it would rake and devour you.

The monster hidden in a child's bedroom.

And . . . it was frightened. It was full of shuddering dread.

She moved forward. She must go to it if she was ever to truly calm it. She moved slowly, creeping and stepping carefully and telling it all the while that all was well.

She heard a noise behind her, the sound of someone else's step and, at that moment, the creature before her turned and fled. Its fear overwhelmed it. It disappeared into the darkness.

Chapter 4

'Honour life.
We are the steg, and the zagle, and the kinfar;
so do not harm life,
save it to keep your own.'

The Song of Lallarop

Parlòp spun round. Taraganam stood behind Krasne, shadowed in the flickering light. The wize woman was standing twelve feet away from her.

'I told you to stay,' said Parlòp angrily.

'You did not return,' said Taraganam. But Parlòp knew she didn't mean it. She had followed because she had desired it. The wize woman did not look sorry. She looked strong and in charge. She had not wanted to wait at the command of a Solpsara. She wanted to be at the forefront of whatever was happening and not a passive spectator. It was going to be difficult to constrain the foolishness of this party.

Taraganam mused to herself. 'That was merely an apparition.'

Parlòp straightened. 'You scared it away. I was trying to pacify it.'

'If it was an apparition, there was no purpose in that.'

Parlòp realised that the wize was talking about something she did not completely comprehend. When the wize talked about their thaumatic art and the casting of unreality she quickly lost interest. So that was the first thing to understand.

'How do you mean . . . an apparition?'

Caresma and the other guard appeared behind her out of the blackness of the stairs and passage. So they too could not wait and had pursued the Karsara woman. Their torches' light flickered and broke the shadows on the walls of the passage, filling the place with unaccustomed light.

'An apparition?' said Caresma. 'So, he left an apparition here? What for? To frighten those who tried to follow him?'

'What is an apparition?' said Parlòp, frustrated. Why did no one listen to her except when they wanted something? Taraganam again ignored the question, staring at the open gateway ahead of them.

Caresma turned lazily to regard Parlòp. He slowly readied himself to answer. 'An apparition . . . well, you would need to appreciate more about the thaumato. There is a darker side to its power. One best avoided.' He gazed at her with the air of a bored schoolmaster teaching a dense and stupid pupil. Clearly, he was wondering if she would be able to understand. 'We cast images, yes? Phantasms into people's perception of the world by the power of our minds. Or we can remove people's perceptions of objects and people around them. Easy, but there are pitfalls in that, which caused many problems in earlier centuries. You see, to do it we must first imagine the phantasy, construct the place we go in and of ourselves. Find the thing we add in our minds, in our ka, our core, our heart as some of the peoples say.'

He looked simultaneously frustrated and confused as he tried to explain. 'To do so we must, well, be in control, we must have our own emotions and feelings unified with our judgment, our reason. If we do not, then we run the risk of other things appearing. Ideas, pictures from other places within us. Thoughts we do not control. The unconscious, the dark side of the ka, where hidden and scared things still lurk and linger – fears, worries, tensions from our lives. They are buried deep within our ka because they were unacceptable, or scary, or disturbing. We must be unified in our ka or these phenomena can come to haunt us. When they come, if a wize is inexperienced, it can be a dark and difficult thing. More importantly, they are uncontrolled. These dark phantasms of our unconscious imagination are called apparitions.'

Taraganam looked back, clearly finding the conversation tiresome. 'We all have nightmares,' she said shortly. 'As children, we conceive the things we fear. They do not depart us. They remain within us, lost in a place we cannot reach. This thing you saw was a child's vision of some nightmare beast. It was a phantom – a shade. But it was uncontrolled.' She turned away, returning to her thoughts.

Caresma said. 'The wize must not let this side, this darkness within control the phantasm or it creates a shadow of our hidden fears. The beast you saw was not there. Skilled as he was, it was an apparition that escaped his ka. Likely, he was not in control of himself. The stress of a moment led him to lose ka unification. Or perhaps he consciously sent it out to scare any who dared follow him – though who or why he feared enough to do that, I cannot think.'

Taraganam walked forward towards the gateway. 'It could not have harmed us, any more than the wall above was real.' She did not look back at Parlòp as she spoke. 'The one you just walked through . . .'

She was eager to go on. Why? What did she know?

Parlòp considered what they had said. It did not entirely gel with the seeming reality of the beast she had faced. If it was a phantasm like the wall, like other images the Kelsar had cast in skirmishes and wars with the swamp, she should not have felt it as an animal – should she? Were the wize capable of tricking the magic of the Solpsar? She thought not. She had felt its mind, its heart, its ka as they put it.

The beast was real. She knew that. Or did . . .?

But she could not ask them, any more than they were revealing their secrets to her. For to do so was to reveal the secrets of the Solpsar. The reality of the connection was well hidden. She must not be the one to break the silence of eight hundred years.

'It felt real.' She settled on that as a comment, weak as it was.

'It wasn't,' said Taraganam brusquely. 'Shall we move on, discover what Kalanomena was seeking here?'

But you know, don't you? Or you suspect.

The wize woman strode forward, hefting her torch and walking purposefully for the gate. 'We must beware of other apparitions awaiting us. They will not be able to harm us . . . but they may be able to trick us.'

'Wait,' said Parlòp.

Taraganam stopped, hesitating in the gateway itself. She looked back, annoyed. 'Well, come on.'

A cry sounded, the cry of a tormented and tortured animal wailing its fear and its anger.

Taraganam flinched in instinctive concern but she spoke out firmly at the same moment. 'It is not real.'

But she sounded less convinced. And there, Parlòp knew, was the true power of the phantasms of the wize. You did not know what was real and what was fantasy. The cry sounded again, more in anger now than fear. This beast did not want them to come. Had this apparition been cast by Kalanomena to frighten those who followed? But what about the claw marks on the body? Had everyone else forgotten them? They were stupid enough.

Parlòp was sure. She didn't believe what they were saying. This impossible animal did exist and Taraganam had scared it and broken her attempt at understanding. Now, its fear had taken it over. Her attempts to calm were cast aside. It was not only afraid. It was angry. Its fear would result in violence if they invaded its domain.

She opened her mouth.

Behind Taraganam a great shadow loomed and she, who had been looking back at the rest of the party, swung around at its arrival. Great claws descended from the darkness of the beast and tore at her shoulders and her head, raking her face. Saimar let out a huge growl and leapt forward with speed quite beyond the normal languorous calm of the allarg.

Parlòp sent out a fierce and imperious order to cease, to them both. The creature yowled its defiance but nonetheless obeyed and disappeared away into the darkness, its shadowy shape lost into the greater darkness beyond. Taraganam collapsed whimpering to the floor, blood gushing from a great gash across her face and right shoulder. Saimar had skittered to a stop just short of Taraganam and turned back to glare at Parlòp, letting out an angry growl at being stopped. His instinct was to attack. To kill before he was killed.

Caresma rushed forward, Krasne following but, just before they reached the fallen wize woman, they seemed to think better of their impulse and slowed to a stop just short of her. The allarg was between them and the Karsar wize. Saimar's tail was lashing and crashing behind him.

Taraganam was lying on one arm, the other reaching up to her face and wincing as her hand touched the raw wound. Blood poured down her hand, her face, and dripped from her chin onto her robes. She would be scarred. Parlòp had no doubt.

'It was there.' She sobbed. 'It was no apparition. Can he have finally accomplished it?'

Parlòp strode past Krasne and Caresma, batting the allarg with her foot to instruct him to move aside. 'What do you know? What was Kalanomena doing here?' she said.

Taraganam wailed again. Krasne stepped past Parlòp and knelt before Taraganam to attend to her. He took things from his bag to tend her wound.

'What is going on here, Taraganam?' Parlòp did not shy from shouting it out, even as a wize suffered before her. 'You know something.' If this accursed Karsara did not reveal what she knew they could all be in very great danger. Why were they so intractable?

'He spoke of an . . .' She cried out again as Krasne, cleaning the wound, produced a needle and scatgut thread.

'You will need to be stitched and cauterised,' he said. 'Or it will become infected and it will scar very badly.'

'He spoke of what?' Parlòp said. 'I have to know.'

Caresma grasped her arm. 'Wait, can't you? She is suffering.'

'We could all be in danger if we do not know what she knows.'

Taraganam looked up. Pushing Krasne's hand aside for a moment, wincing, she said, 'He was obsessed with the idea of a forming... a maker... an apparatus capable of actual creation. A device that could make an eidetic real. Make it actually there. Fabricate permanently. He was consumed by the ambition for it. He spent weeks researching the concept, he read old texts of the ancient times when the magician kings had many skills we have lost.' She stopped and waved Krasne back into care for her wound.

'A maker...?' said Caresma. 'Even the ancients did not speak of such a thing. They did not know how to materialise the imagination of the thaumato into the actuality of the world. It would require too much energy. What would the source be?' He stopped as if, once again, realising that he had said too much.

And Parlòp thought that he had again spoken of things that he understood but they did not.

'Energy? Like energeia?' she said. 'I have heard ancient stories of powerful magic to capture and utilise energy to destroy things. It is no longer in the world. What do you speak of? Why do you need energy to do this?'

Caresma looked disgruntled. He knew he had spoken without thought but he must have understood that he could not escape answering some questions. 'An ancient text I once read... lost, I fear now... said that energy and matter were the same thing in different forms. So energy could be formed from matter and matter from energy. I did not understand it fully.' He looked uncomfortable.

He was lying. He did understand it.

Caresma went on, slowing. 'So to make an imagined cast of thaumato into reality . . . you would surely need a massive energy source.'

Parlòp realised that this did not fully answer the questions that flooded her mind, but she could also see from Caresma's expression that he would now dissemble and lie his way out of his unfortunate revelations. He would divulge no more.

'So Kalanomena created this nightmare, this apparition into reality,' she said. 'Why would he do that?'

Krasne was finished sewing and gently cauterising the wound with a tinder-rod. He was now dressing her wound.

Taraganam spoke painfully. 'Apparitions are not cast intentionally, ever. It is part of the discipline of a wize to not cast the nightmares or shadows from our darkness. When we do we do not control them because they are born of a part of us that is uncontrolled. We curb ourselves. We unify our ka. We cast only what we wish to cast – what serves our lords. If he cast a nightmare dream from his childhood – which that seemed to be – he did not do it intentionally. His core had fractured. He was unchecked. He had failed. His unity was lost.'

Caresma spoke. 'But we cannot leave such a creature roaming these rooms.' He looked decisive but Parlòp knew there was another aim here. What was it? Caresma went on. 'Krasne, send Barces up to bring one of the other two guards and send the other back to the Kelsari. We will need more soldiers.' He stepped forward. 'We cannot leave that creature. With this way open it could escape into the world whenever it wishes. Once it was free, think of the havoc it could wreak in Kel'Katoh, in the world. It must be stopped.'

'Are we enough?' said Parlòp.

'We must be. We are two wize who can confuse it with thaumatic phantasms. We have an allarg. There are guards with swords. Surely we can bring it down if we work together. Chrasm, our Kelsari, will send more troops. But we cannot wait for them. It might escape at any time.'

Parlòp noted that he left her out of his list of useful people – except as the bringer of an allarg. She was just a weak swamp woman and all knew that the Solpsar were useless apart from the beasts they trained. They did not know the true power of the swamp.

Caresma had paused dramatically. 'We cannot allow a beast constructed of Kalanomena's nightmare to roam the world. This is why the wize had to learn to unify their ka. To control what is projected is key. If we can create the phantasms into the actual, it is even more essential, or the world could descend into madness.' He drew a shuddering breath. 'Imagine it. This apparition must be stopped and the apparatus . . . or the magic by which he achieved this must be destroyed.'

Taraganam surged to her feet. 'No. Think instead of the good that could come of such a gift! The ability to remake the world, to provide all that is required. We could bring back the ancient times, the glories of the reign of the magician kings. We could repair the world from the ravaging of the makkuz, the Hraddas monsters of the skies. And we could do it just by imagining it.'

'It will be harder than that,' Caresma shouted angrily, and the two wize began to bicker again. Parlòp ignored them and stepped away, looking meaningfully at Krasne. The officer did not respond but instead spoke brief, quiet words to Barces who, taking the opportunity, ran quickly away back up the passageway. Parlòp assumed he had sent him for aid and to order a guard to return to the Kelsari and bring further troops as Caresma had ordered.

Parlòp walked past the two arguing wize and stood just before the gate. Saimar quickly scuttled to stand alongside her. She voiced him her gratitude and then stretched out her magic of understanding away into the darkness beyond, seeking the shadow beast.

She knew this beast was frightened. It was, she now realised, composed of fear. It was constructed of Kalanomena's dread – the nightmare of the child he had been. It had escaped his mind but now it existed for itself. But surely it deserved something better than swift destruction. It was not to blame for its nature, not to blame for its existence. No animal was. No plant was to blame for being the thing it was, where it was. This apparition had not caused itself to be made or made as it was. It did not deserve death.

She could not sense it. The beast was nowhere near. This was a puzzle.

Parlòp wondered how far these passages and tunnels stretched. They were far below the ruins of Vyderbo now. She had imagined they were just in a few caverns hollowed out of the rock on which it stood. What if they were deeper than that, below even the river? *These tunnels could go anywhere.* The very thought shocked her.

What if there is another exit? Then the beast could indeed escape.

She turned and looked back, beyond the arguing wize, to Krasne. The guard was standing still, his bag thrust once more behind him and his sword drawn, ready. He, like her, liked to act and not just to talk. She stared at him. Did he understand that all this was not as clear and simple as the wize had stated? There was something to be done here but it was not at all clear what.

Parlòp looked back at the wize, squabbling still.

'Are we doing this?' she said, strident, cutting across their argument. 'Each moment that you argue the beast is getting further away.'

Taraganam turned to glare at her. Her face was swollen, angry and raw where the beast had clawed her. 'What do you mean?'

'The beast has moved away. I can tell.' She paused. 'These tunnels might be larger than we thought. It could escape. What makes you think this is the only way in or out?'

Caresma looked appalled.

At that moment Barces arrived with the other guard, Tarsh. 'I have sent Wasama for reinforcements, sir,' he said to Krasne.

'We will need them,' said Caresma.

'Tarsh. Draw your weapon and be alert,' said Krasne.

Caresma straightened and turned away from Taraganam. He touched the side of his head and, seemingly springing from nothing, more and more guards appeared, all simple variations on the three riverguards they actually had. In moments it appeared they had an army with them. He had cast a thaumatic phantasm.

'The beast will think twice about striking against us now,' he said confidently. 'So, let us start the hunt.'

Parlòp sighed. This was going to end badly.

A Crystals Prequel in the Singer Series

Chapter 5

'There is no difference in life
– tree, animal and person.
You are them.'

The Song of the Triffer

For a pregnant moment, no one moved. None of them wanted to be the one at the front of the party. So Parlòp decided.

Briskly, she hefted her torch, growled a summoning to Saimar and walked. Reaching the gate, she stepped through. It opened onto a wide and spacious hall, its roof held up by four great stone pillars. At first, she saw no other exits or entrances in the flickering light of her torch cascading into the darkness. She looked up at the roof far above. The skills of the maven who built this place amazed her. Not only had they built all this underground, but who could build such a high vaulted ceiling with pillars so tall and sturdy? But then, she thought, they were the same people who had built Vyderbo. And that building above that towered to four storeys high. She understood how to create that by guiding the growth of ancient trees. But how could you fashion it in stone?

The light of her torch did not reach the furthest end of the room or its edge. There was no sign of the shadow beast in the hall, but the corners remained dim suggestions, vague presences lost in darkness. The beast could have been hiding in the gloom. But she no longer sensed its presence. It was further away, in some place beyond this. Forgotten in the blackness, lost to its fear and scared of what they might do to it because of its impulsive attack. She was sure it had not meant to kill. It had attacked from instinct, as a cornered frightened animal always would. A need to strike before being struck.

Parlòp raised her torch higher. She realised there was a great construction in stone in the centre of the hall. Might it have been a fountain long ago? The room appeared to contain little else. It looked like the vestibule of a great palace, to welcome new arrivals before whisking them on to greater rooms and more important people. Had the ancestors of the Kelsar lived here? Why then had its very existence been forgotten? Or was it something else entirely? If so, what had it been?

'What are these vaults, do you think?' said Taraganam, speaking Parlòp's thoughts from just a step behind her. 'Why did you not know they were here, under the ruins?' She turned and looked quite pointedly at Caresma.

The Fount of the Kelsar shrugged. 'It is eight hundred years since ancient times came to an end. Much has been forgotten in the world. There was a lot of chaos and disorder in the early years after the ravaging. Some say that more died in the turmoil than in the attack of the makkuz from the stars. The world was broken. Ideas, thoughts, wisdom and knowledge died with that generation. The Kelsar would not be alone in forgetting many things.'

'And what is this chamber for?' said Krasne. Parlòp turned and looked at him. Many guards were standing behind him. It took her a few moments to identify the forms of the real Barces and Tarsh amongst the phantasms. Parlòp wondered if these illusions would be of any use in a real fight with the shadow beast. Would it even be fooled by them as people would? Most animals were cleverer than that.

'It looks like an antechamber,' said Taraganam. 'Just an area where people waited and were greeted. It would indicate that there is a great deal more to these vaults. It was why I asked the question.' She sounded ill-tempered. Perhaps her wound hurt.

Parlòp moved slowly forward. Their verbosity would continue but it would contribute little. Saimar moved with her and she reached the fountain and held her torch up to look around the room. She heard someone move to stand behind her and, turning, saw that it was Krasne. The others were still standing further back, nearer the gate, and safety.

She looked at them talking and then walked slowly past the empty fountain. Beyond it, at the far end of the hall, was a great archway and beyond that, steps led down to the left. She hesitated. She could feel that the shadow beast was there, waiting, further down the stairs, close to the next landing below. It had fled from them and run down. But then it had stopped because it feared what was below more than it feared them. She held out a hand to stop Krasne from going any further. But it appeared that the officer was happy for her to lead. Was that self-preservation or did he appreciate she was the best person? She crouched, attending to the feelings of the creature ahead of them.

This beast was miserable. She felt its emotions pouring out. It despaired of its very existence. It was cringing on the stairs, unable to cope with the vision of its future. It had no hope. Parlòp voiced it, trying to heal some of the damage. She did not know what had hurt it. Was it some event that made it so lost? Or was it done by whoever had created it? But, in the end, she did not mind. It was not important. It was a beast and it was in an abject state. That was not acceptable.

If she did not act then the whole crowd of them would thoughtlessly march down and that would result in another confrontation. Even if not, it could result in the beast fleeing from them, distressed and panicking even more. That would only deepen its sense of despair. It would result, when it was finally cornered, in extreme violence. People would be killed. The beast itself could die. She must prevent that. If not for the sake of more wounding and potentially death, then for the sake of the beast.

'Let's check the edges of this hall,' she said loudly. 'We do not want any threats behind us as we proceed.'

Krasne nodded his agreement and, turning, he signalled to his two guards. He turned and moved quickly to meet them. Parlòp rose to her feet and moved to the right, heading for the wall. As she went the light of her torch spilt into the dark shadows of the room. There were carvings on the wall, similar in style to the bas-reliefs that had covered the walls through which Kalanomena had smashed his way. They were striking, filling the whole of the wall.

She looked back. Her scheme had worked. Krasne had ordered his guards to search the room and the phantasms created by Caresma were all seemingly doing the same thing, scattering through the room. Caresma was walking towards the far wall too. She could not tell his intentions. Taraganam was now standing alone in the centre of the hall next to the fountain, staring fixedly forward. She had seen the stairway downward and wanted, desperately, for them to get on with descending. She was still hiding something about her knowledge of this place, or the intent of Kalanomena in coming here. But then, she had seemed as surprised as them all to find the vaults. It was a puzzle that needed solving.

From where she stood, Parlòp voiced the beast, sending calm and care to it, trying to give it some sort of emotional stability. It responded to her. Perhaps for the first time, she believed that it would be calm enough to come to summoning and be open to understanding. She could help it. It would begin to achieve some peace in its existence.

She voiced it to keep ahead of them, to not oppose them as they descended. That resulted in a blast of agitation, fear of what lay below, terror of what would threaten it there. It was too frightened to show her what it was. She could not understand. But she knew the beast had heard her voice. It would not attack. She must keep it ahead of them until she could calm it. Then, despite its fear, she could summon it to her. Nothing would happen unless the others trapped it.

She turned her attention to the carvings on the wall. She must try and understand what they depicted. Perhaps knowledge of them, of this place, would aid them in comprehending what they faced. What was it Kalanomena had sought? What power had he found here to create the beast? And even if the claw marks on his body were those of the shadow creature, what had cast the fire had burnt him as he fled?

She held her torch higher. The giant frieze showed pictures of the ancient world, she was sure of it. The people in the bas-reliefs were ordinary enough, their clothes not outlandish. They were doing things, but she could not tell what. They held strange devices. There were staffs, but they held other things she could not identify, flat things that did not look like books or scrolls. Beyond the figures, sculpted with great skill, were many buildings. She was amazed at the height of them. People said that there were tall buildings far away in the lands of the Lake people. The city of In Haxass was said to be deeply impressive to see, an echo of former times. But even the wildest tales of the palaces of the Aallesar did not compare with these great edifices. Also, there were things in the skies above them that could have been birds, but Parlòp had never seen birds like these. They must be some wonder of the ancient magician kings.

She turned back. It was safe; they could descend. The beast had been warned to stay ahead of them There would be no conflict and no violent end to a pitiable creature's existence. By exploring this place they could discover why Kalanomena had come.

She gazed around the room. The others had followed her example. They were searching the room diligently for clues and threats. Only Taraganam remained motionless, standing gazing at the steps ahead waiting impatiently for them to proceed. She gazed with an intensity that spoke of deep emotion. Parlòp could not read it. Excitement perhaps, or fear? Eagerness to attain something? Whatever it was, Parlòp was now ready to descend too. She had her own secret aim – to rescue the shadow beast.

Just as Parlòp stepped forward to speak to Taraganam, Barces cried out and plucked an object from the centre of the empty fountain. Those searching the room swung round, such was the urgency of the cry. Parlòp walked rapidly over to him. When she was within an arm's length, she saw what he held. She had never seen such a device. It was a long hollow tube with what looked like a small cudgel at one end.

'What is it?' said Taraganam, turning back, away from gazing at the steps.

Was it just a strangely shaped mace? But why leave the long tubular handle hollow? She stopped. *Or was it even the handle?* She could see a lever at the bottom of the tube, beside the bulbous club. Barces was holding the tube up to his eyes and peering down inside it. No doubt he was trying, in the torchlight, to see if there was anything inside.

'Be careful,' said Caresma shortly. 'You do not know what it is.'

The Fount had stepped forward to take the device. But Krasne, standing beside Barces, moved faster and snatched the device from the loosened fingers of the riverguard. Without a word, he promptly grasped the club end. He had decided it was the handle. He stepped forward, beside Taraganam, and pointed at the open stairwell. He pulled the lever with a finger.

A great burning spurt of yellow fire emerged from the tube and flashed across the intervening space, like lightning filling the sky. The whole hall was revealed. Saimar snarled. Krasne had been careful. There was no one in the way. He released the lever and the burning fire ceased. Parlòp felt the shadow beast panic. It moved several steps further down and then, as its fear overtook it, it came back up. What was below that scared it so much?

Caresma grunted.

Holding her torch up to see better in the returned gloom, Parlòp looked over at the stairwell her sight dulled by the sudden light.

The wall of the landing beyond was blackened and some of it had even melted.

Some instinct, some suspicion made her turn and look back at the gateway through which they had come. Then she saw it. They had not noticed because they had been intent on moving into the hall, heading forwards. There were more burnt areas around that archway. Something, someone had fired this device at that entrance too.

She realised what that could mean.

'This device is how Kalanomena died. Look . . .' she said and pointed back at the gate. They all looked in that direction and regarded the blackened and burnt walls. Then as one they turned and gazed back at the firestick device in Krasne's hands.

'Someone killed him with this.' Krasne held it up, awe in his voice. 'But if he died here and the killer abandoned this device, throwing it into the fountain, how did his body get back up to the surface? Surely after being struck by such a fierce fire he could not have survived long enough to run or crawl all that way.'

'Not with the extent of the burns on his body,' said Taraganam. 'Caresma and I examined them. Maybe these blasts did not hit him. His assailant missed and hit the walls. Then they, whoever they were, continued to pursue him up to the surface, still blasting after him with this fire.'

'We saw no other damage on the way down,' said Krasne.

'Yes, there was,' said Parlòp. 'On the second landing.' But no one was listening to her.

'If they killed him in the city square, why bring it back here to throw it carelessly away? Indeed, why come back here at all? Why not escape?'

'Perhaps he did die in these vaults and another person carried him up to the surface, away from his killer,' said Parlòp, but she had the feeling no one heard. They weren't listening to her. She sighed. Yet this was the role of a mystic – to discover, to understand and to teach. It was, supposedly, the reason they had called for her to come. Now they didn't care what she thought. This was typical of runnelers – conceited.

She turned and gazed back at the far stairwell. She still felt the beast below, waiting, misery swirling through its being. Despite its fear, there was a kindness there too, deep within it, a bizarre gentleness in such a viciously fashioned creature. The shadow creature had strange integrity – the nobility of the vulnerable.

Then . . . she understood.

Had the beast carried his body up to the surface? Did that explain the claw marks on the front of the corpse? He was killed in these vaults as he fled. Kalanomena had created the beast. Would it have held some regard for him, enough to care, enough to bear him away from his murderer? Had it grasped his corpse in its great talons and run from the killer, escaping with the dead body of the man whose ka had given it birth? It would explain much. Parlòp let the thoughts settle. Yes, she was sure of it.

She did not bother to share her ideas.

'So there is someone else down here,' said Caresma, 'who chased and killed Kalanomena with this . . . firestick.' He looked very earnest. 'We have more than one enemy down here to pursue. The apparition beast of his childhood nightmares and whoever killed him with that.' He indicated the gadget with a careless wave of his hand. Parlòp had the feeling the Fount already knew more of the firestick than he said. She sensed a falseness to the gesture and in his portrayed emotions.

Was she alone in seeing his deception?

'Should we go on? Or wait for the extra riverguards to arrive?' said Krasne. 'Is this not too risky?'

'We should go on,' said Taraganam swiftly.

'We must continue,' Caresma said equally rapidly. 'Who knows what may happen if we do not? Nothing has changed. We do not know the extent of these vaults. There may be ways for both the beast and the killer to escape. We must try to prevent that. More death will result if we hold back. The Kelsari will come. We sent the guard Wasama to fetch him. He will follow in force.'

Parlòp did not bother to chip in. Both the wize, Caresma and Taraganam, were playing some deeper game here. But whatever it was, she too knew they must go on. If she let them wait for the Kelsari and a larger number of guards, they would all be intent on the shadow beast's destruction. It would make her task of calming it and summoning it impossible.

She called to Saimar, who was laying lazily by the fountain. She walked swiftly through the archway and onto the first landing. She looked to the left, down the stairs. She felt the beast below skittering downwards, warned by her presence. They were coming.

Its panic was pathetic. She must protect this creature, whatever the cost. It did not deserve hatred. It was constructed of one man's fears. Neither its appearance nor its nature were its fault.

To discover, to understand and to teach. And to protect.

She heard the others hurrying to follow her. She did not wait but stepped sideways to let Saimar come beside her and walked down the stairs. The glimmering light of her torch showed another landing some fifty or so feet below. There, the stairs turned. She felt this was where the shadow beast had cowered, too scared of what was beneath. Yet frightened of them as well.

She walked briskly down as if there was nothing to fear. But shivers of apprehension went down her spine as she considered what might be ahead. She reached the landing and turned left, back on herself. The next room would be under the hall above them. So these vaults were built below each other. How far down would they go?

She briefly looked back at the party following. Krasne was in the lead with his two guards, then Taraganam and Caresma and finally the illusionary guards followed behind. Without speaking, she descended again towards another landing and the stairs turned right there. That should be a room, below the hall above.

She sensed a strange bestiality ahead, where the stairs ended. It did not seem to be animals – not beasts like Saimar or the shadow. They were confused, one with another. The bestiality had a commonality that she was not used to feeling. She sensed individuals, even a large number, but they were all part of the same. Insects? It was . . . it was a sea of animalism.

It was confusing. But she could not warn the others without divulging her magic. She walked slowly downwards, trying as she did to better sense what it was.

She reached the bottom and turned to see an archway. She lifted her torch so that its light spilt into the room beyond. The sight took her breath away. The room was filled with monstrous forms, moving wordlessly and soundlessly screaming. They were half female and half beast. One had a woman's face with the body of a ligon, and then the long, sensuous tail of a serpent. Another was an animal head on a woman's torso with insect legs. The next was a beast yet with all the parts and form of a woman.

She understood then what she had sensed. These creatures were not distinct. They moved. They had being. Yet they were not individual but common, an ocean of sensual bestiality. They were not animals. They were not people either. They were alive but yet not. They were not one among many but many that were one.

Whatever they were, they were hopelessly lost in squalor. They were just constructs of another terrible dream. If the ka of Kalanomena had fractured to produce the shadow beast of his nightmares, his increasing derangement had produced fantasies of desire and bestiality, combining the two in horrific ways.

The female faces resembled the strong, powerful features of Taraganam and the female forms of their bodies were an exaggerated and overstated version of her form.

The wize was standing beside Parlòp. 'Kill them,' she said.

'Destroy them all!'

As she spoke a great dark gruesome hakkat burst into being. At once, it threw itself into attacking the repulsive half-woman-half-beasts writhing ahead of them. Yet it did not connect.

Parlòp realised there was no new threat. It was a phantasm birthed of Taraganam's anger. She was incensed, deeply upset and offended.

'Calm yourself!' said Caresma from behind. 'Centre your ka. We need no further apparitions to follow us here.'

'Destroy them,' she repeated tightly. 'Kill them. Annihilate them all. They are an offence!' But even as her anger raged, the phantasm swinging hopelessly at the forms before them faded and she let out a long, exasperated breath, hissing between her teeth.

There came a terrible roar from beyond the darkness.

Parlòp raised her torch. It was not the shadow beast. It was something that Parlòp could not sense. What further horrendous nightmare was ahead? Was it what the shadow beast had feared in descending?

Saimar snarled a loud challenge. But Parlòp realised that the new monstrosity was not roaring at them. It was threatening the shadow. The beast was being attacked and was skittering and dodging to avoid whatever it was. She voiced sympathy and support.

The beast was trying to escape. Parlòp was distraught.

The unknown monster roared its defiance and wrath.

Chapter 6

> *'On the heights,*
> *beside the way,*
> *at the crossroads the teaching took its stand;*
> *beside the gates of the town,*
> *at the entrance of the portals it taught:*
> *"To you, I call and my cry is to all life."'*
>
> *The Book of Sirath*

Taraganam seized the firestick. She plucked it from Krasne's hands. He did not react fast enough to stop her.

She turned it rapidly. Yellow fire streamed from the tube. It quickly enveloped the nearest humiliating form. It had her face but the body of a sensuous writhing beast. It burst into flame, screaming soundlessly as it burned away into nothingness. The fire consumed it as if it was formed of paper and not flesh.

She was already killing the next one.

Parlòp did not care.

Ahead, in the light of the blazing stream of yellow flame, was the new monstrosity. She paled. At the furthest end of the huge chamber, it slowly, almost gently, turned to face them. It had the form of a kinfar, the great beasts of the plain the Torasar tended. But it was changed.

'What have you done!' shouted Caresma.

This was no docile eater of grass. Parlòp saw great curved, vicious horns, two on each side. They were fierce and terrible in their sharpness. The kinfar-beast had a tail like a grotesque snake with a barbarous sting on its end. It had been roaring its wrath through the far archway, which must have descended to even greater depths. Something had escaped its wrath by running through the arch.

The shadow beast had fled. But the horror of a kinfar had not been able to get through to pursue it. It was too large. How had it even come here? Must it, like the demeaning forms of women, have been created?

The light from the firestick had faded. Taraganam had stopped firing or had been stopped. Krasne had snatched the firestick from Taraganam's grasp. She let go of it, staring, open-mouthed.

Parlòp could no longer see the kinfar-horror. It had been wrapped in darkness. A slow, tentative, curious growl sounded from the far end of the great hall. Silence. A terrible pause and then a louder, more wrathful roar. She heard it move. It was coming.

Slowly out of the blackness, the horror of a kinfar appeared into the torchlight. It tensed like a predator readying to strike – a bull kinfar readying to charge.

'Kill it!' screamed Caresma. The phantasms of guards he had created all ran forward as one to confront the beast, to make it hesitate, to give it pause long enough for them to—

The horror moved very fast. Faster than any stampeding kinfar, it leapt across the room. It charged unceremoniously through the illusions. Had it even perceived them? Krasne dodged abruptly to the right and, dropping to the ground, rolled away. Parlòp moved left – summoning Saimar to follow. Caresma and Taraganam threw themselves to the right after Krasne. Tarsh ran left, after Parlòp.

Barces was just a step behind, but he did not move fast enough. He was drawing his sword as the horror, head bowed and horns extended, reached him. The horns impaled him, ripping through his flesh. It shook him viciously, an animal killing its prey, and then threw him down. Great jaws closed around his head and shoulders. He was seized in its terrible jagged teeth – not the teeth of a docile kinfar.

He was snapped in two. His abdomen, loins and legs flew off

into the chamber as it shook his head. Blood spurted, fountaining up into the air. The horror did not chase. It crunched down on Barces' torso and turned towards Tarsh and Parlòp.

Krasne was up then, on his knees. Fire blasted from the firestick. Yellow light filled the whole chamber again. Flames burst into being on the back of the fiendish kinfar. Its hair caught alight, burning with fierce redness. The world was filled with light, blood spattering and filling the chamber with gore. The stink of burning, charred flesh filled the air. Its great head turned from Tarsh and Parlòp to consider its fiery attacker. It moved with a strange grace as if its back was not burning. Krasne fired again as its head swung round.

Parlòp, behind the creature now, ordered Saimar to attack. The allarg leapt forward joyously, freed of her constraint. His great teeth closed around the great serpent tail of the horror and his powerful jaw closed. The squelch of ripping flesh and the snap of breaking bones echoed round the chamber. The horror hesitated, swinging to find the new attacker. Saimar moved quickly. Lashing his great tail he snapped at the back of the creature.

Krasne fired And yellow flames filled the air. The head of the beast caught alight, a hot stench filled the air. Red flames leapt upwards from its head. The horror staggered. Saimar leapt away, out of its reach, his jaws closing over the back leg of the creature. The allarg pulled back, ripping the leg from the body, and blood erupted out in a great fountain of foulness.

Is this thing alive?

How had she not sensed it? Had its presence been lost to her in that ocean of sensual bestiality around them? She ordered Saimar back and he retreated reluctantly, flesh hanging from his maw.

The horror stumbled back and swung, striking out wildly, crushing one of the animalistic forms and ripping the female body from the tigon head. Weak now, it tottered. Krasne continued to bathe it in yellow fire. It staggered, burning, filling the air with the stench of death, writhing in torment. It released a painful and wretched bellow and fell towards the arch, its great horns breaking the top of the archway. The keystone shattered and the horror collapsed into the stairwell. The stones of the arch and then the roof smashed down onto the head of the monstrous kinfar, which hit the ground with a soggy, heavy squelch. It screamed an agony of suffering as rocks piled down upon it.

Then its wrath was passed, lost in yellow fire and burning flesh.

Its head and shoulders were through the arch. More of the arch and roof fell onto it and the walls collapsed inwards. The way was blocked. Its body and tail remained on their side, burning with savage fire.

Whatever it was, whatever it had been, however it had been created, it had trapped them. It was dead. Krasne had defeated it. But it had killed them in return – the way back was completely closed. They could not get out.

They were stunned for many moments, unable to move. They had all dropped their torches in the panic. The chamber was lit now only by the light of the burning monster.

Krasne cursed. 'What was that?'

'I . . . don't . . .' Taraganam stammered out some incoherency.

'Barces is dead,' said Tarsh. It was not anger. It was shock.

Krasne strode forward. He picked up the torch he had dropped. It sputtered and splattered sparks out. He held it up, the flame became stronger and more light filled the chamber.

Parlòp was kneeling beside her allarg. Saimar was not hurt – he was eating the chunk of flesh he had torn from the leg of the kinfar. The crunching sound echoed around them. Parlòp leaned forward, worried what poison he might be eating. But the flesh, such as she could see, looked sound. Saimar would not have released it to her. There were limits to what a healthy allarg would do when it came to food, even for her order. Animals were controlled by the Solpsar in the knowing and understanding of their instinctive nature.

Her torch was on the floor next to her. It had gone out. She plucked it from the ground and, leaving the allarg to his small feast, walked over to where Krasne was standing, still shocked by the horror of what had just happened. She put her torch to his and the fire guttered and spluttered to life.

Taraganam was standing motionless staring at the burning monster they had killed. She said nothing.

Tarsh swore at her. 'You provoked that thing. You killed Barces.' He moved towards her as if to strike her down, his sword was in his hand.

'Tarsh, stop!' Krasne's tone was uncompromising – an officer in charge, a soldier to control.

'But he died!' screamed Tarsh. 'He died because she angered . . . that thing.' But he stopped. He did not strike the Karsara woman.

'Yes, he died,' said Krasne. 'And that is the role of a guard. You know this. To fight and die. We all take the oath.'

Tarsh gave a sobbing snarl and turned away.

'We need to pause,' said Caresma. 'We must regroup, rethink our position.'

Krasne, ignoring Caresma's words, swung round and shot the firestick at the remains of Barces' legs, which were incinerated to ash under the long blast. 'May your ashes float to the Great Bight of the ancestors.'

'Stop firing that,' said Caresma. 'We may need its power ahead of this.'

Krasne turned and gazed at the Fount without a speck of agreement on his face.

'Does it have limits then?' said Parlòp curiously.

Caresma turned his head towards her lazily, not caring that he might, again, have revealed a deeper understanding of the device than anyone else. 'Probably,' he said eventually. 'Most things do.'

Without warning Tarsh, his sword drawn, advanced to kill the remaining forms of Kalanomena's lascivious desires. His sword rose and fell as he destroyed them rhythmically. They did not resist the slaughter but just looked up at the swinging sword of death. No one stopped him until every one of the strange forms lay wounded and broken on the floor. Some of them continued to writhe, even when he had sliced them into many pieces. But slowly, as if the strange life that had filled them eked away, they slowed, stopped and perished. The sea of their life, if that was what it had been, was drained.

Parlòp raised her torch and looked around them. She walked into the centre of the huge chamber in which they stood, stepping around and over the dead forms. There were doorways, she realised, open on both sides of the chamber. There must be other rooms here. She sighed and wondered if further horrors awaited them there. At the furthest end of the left-hand wall, one door was closed. It was formed of metal and looked impregnable.

For a moment she doubted her prior certainty that they needed to keep descending. Now Barces was dead and their exit was blocked by the dead kinfar-horror. *We are trapped.* But the only way to get out now was to proceed downwards, to solve the mystery and hope, somehow, that it provided an escape.

But also, the Kelsari knew they were here. He had resources. He would surely dig them out – hopefully before they starved to death. Surely, he could not leave representatives of neighbouring peoples to die. That really would start a war for him on two fronts.

'If we burn it, will we be able to get out?' said Krasne.

Caresma stepped forward. 'Do not use the firestick! There may be other dangers . . .' He stopped. 'Anyway, I'm not sure it would work. It might bring more of the roof down too.'

'Yes, the roof would collapse,' said Parlòp, looking back.

'Then how do we get out? Are we trapped?'

They began to argue. Parlòp left them to it.

She walked cautiously over to the doorway nearest her. She thrust the torch into the opening, expecting it to reveal some horror, but it did not. It was just another room stretching away from her, only ten feet or so deep. She could see little in it but the walls were lined with sets of metal drawers. They were all open and the drawers themselves scattered around. Someone had searched the room but, it seemed to her, this had been done long ago. Despite their proximity to the river, it was quite dry in these vaults. Even so, some of the drawers had slight rust. Everywhere was covered with a deep layer of dust. They were old.

She pulled back out of the doorway and glanced back at the knot of people still examining their blocked exit and bemoaning the lack of an easy return. They weren't decisive people even when the situation was clear – typical.

She moved along the wall to the next open doorway and, again gingerly, put her torch into the opening. This way opened out into a larger room that stretched back into the darkness. Even in her torchlight, she could see large solid stone workbenches crossing the room in rows. The place had the air of a workroom, where centuries before many maven had busied themselves on projects and examinations. At least, that was what she imagined.

Was that what this whole place was, some bizarrely grandiose workplace? An underground vault where the magician kings and their mavens worked to produce the marvels with which they had filled the world.

She had not imagined the Malasar magicians and the Willsar maven like that. She had, rather unconsciously, assumed they achieved all their magical wonders by effortless arcane means. She never thought before that they needed a place to work on them. It was a strange thought, which gave her pause. Perhaps she did not properly understand the nature of their magic.

She took a few steps into the room so that the light of her torch revealed more of the room. It was very large. The light did not reach the far side of the room, and the workbenches or stands stretched away from her in the blackness. She walked further in, passing between them. The floor beneath her feet was covered in debris and other detritus of age. She stepped over it, being careful not to damage her feet on anything sharp. She walked quite a bit further before she was able to see the far wall. Lining it were cupboards and drawers, the drawers were larger than those in the first room. There were what appeared to be display cases above them. Their glass, fragile with age, was broken and smashed. Whatever had been in the display cabinets was gone. Someone had smashed it to get in, but whether recently or long ago she could not tell.

Parlòp crossed the enormous room, stepping between the workbenches and past the remnants of a historic loss. She stopped and stood before the display cases. The dust was very disturbed before one of the cases and here the ancient glass shards were on top of the new trails in the dust. She saw glass on the floor too, lying above the debris of a bygone age. It looked as if this case had been broken more recently. So, she wondered, what had it contained?

Metal clips were fixed on the back of the case.

Had this contained the firestick? Fastened here – on display? By why place such a weapon inside a glass case? It puzzled her as an idea, but the disposition of the clips fitted the rough size of the device. But, assumption as it was, she would never know for sure. Whatever had been displayed in the case, it was gone.

The light behind her brightened and she turned to see Caresma entering the chamber on the far side, holding his torch aloft. He gazed at her with a strangely unreadable expression on his face. He strode forward, quickly crossing the room towards her, scattering dust and debris as he came. He stopped some feet away.

'What are you doing?' he said.

She shrugged. 'Exploring...' She paused. 'Talk gets us nowhere. The only way out of here is to solve this riddle and hope the solution gives us understanding. Waiting for the Kelsari to dig us out will take too long.' She looked at him. 'Before we starve to death.'

Caresma walked towards her. 'We agree, pretty much... out there.' He lowered his torch, its light flickering eerily around his strong features. 'But Krasne disagrees. He argues that we need to be cautious. We do not know what further dangers there are.'

She heard an edge to his voice, which made her think he meant her and this unsanctioned exploration.

'I was careful,' she said and instantly regretted the defensive-sounding words. 'There is little here anyway. The place was emptied long ago. Probably when Vyderbo was ruined... during the ravaging.'

'They did not take everything, it seems,' he said. 'The firestick was here and there is whatever means our killer is using to create all these... coalesced eidetic phantasms.' He had an awkward look as if the phrase was not rigorous enough for him. As if, Parlòp wondered, he had wanted to say something else.

She turned on her heel and strode back, reaching him and moving quickly past. 'Then let's explore the other rooms on this level together.'

Caresma was forced to follow her. She heard him hurrying to catch her up. He did not like being bested by a swamp woman. He was a Kelsara, after all – and a man.

She exited the room. The others were still standing around the carcass of the fiendish kinfar that had attacked them. She decided they were still quarrelling.

She disregarded them. The truth was obvious. Saimar, having finished devouring his pieces of the kinfar, was dozing in the centre of the room. He gazed up at her as she passed, not because he intended to move but in case she was calling him. Seeing that she was not, he closed his eyes to sleep.

Beasts have much to teach us, she thought.

The next room, further along the same wall, was closed. This was the door constructed of metal and so it had survived. She had assumed it would be locked and probably unopenable with the minor implements they had. She walked up to it without much hope that she would ever open it. But as she neared she saw, below the handle, where perhaps a lock had been there was a hole around an inch in diameter.

Caresma appeared at her side. She indicated it all to him and then, without pausing further, grasped the handle and pulled it back. Their torchlight filled a small room lined with small metal cupboards, floor to ceiling. They were all open and emptied. But one of them had been smashed open and again, Parlòp thought, the signs were that this was recent. She moved to it and, stretching upwards, peered inside to see nothing but a small metal box. It had been opened and then thrown untidily back into the cupboard. Caresma beside her was taller and was looking into it over her shoulder. She gave him a significant look. He did not speak.

Parlòp knew there was nothing to say. They would never know for certain what was inside this small cabinet. But, like the display case, it made Parlòp suspicious. It looked as if, very recently, somebody had found something. She wondered what it was. They had found the firestick, used it, and abandoned it and found something else here. What new shocking horror would that be? The means to produce these solid dreams? To give reality to the kinfar monster?

Deftly stepping past Caresma, she walked back out of the small room into the main area. The rest of the party had stopped discussing how to dig their way back out and were settling. Tarsh was now guarding the arch that led down. It was sensible. They did not want any threats to come up without warning. Back along the wall, Taraganam and Krasne were peering unhappily into the first of the rooms that Parlòp had explored.

Parlòp, along with Caresma, walked past Tarsh over to the far side of the great chamber to the doorway opposite them. She remembered that there were only two doorways on that wall. The first of them led to an even larger room than any she'd explored. She stared inside. It was full of large metal cabinets. They were strange cabinets because there were no doors and there was some sort of racking inside as if there had been something slid into them but long removed. Remains of other furniture were strewn on the floor. Despite the dryness of the air of the vaults, they had long collapsed to dust and debris. It was impossible to guess what they had once been. She walked past the empty racking cupboards to the back of the room. When she reached it her torch revealed more exits. They were all open, the doors long ago rotted and gone, leading to a maze of small rooms off several corridors. She patiently explored them all, with Caresma walking beside her. She found nothing in them but the remnants of things long perished into withered destruction. The next doorway led to a similar maze of little rooms, long emptied of anything but dust and debris.

It had, for her, still the air of a place of work. But why build a workplace so far below ground? Had there been no space in the huge city of Vyderbo to work? It puzzled her. It was not a palace as she had first thought. It was a place of study and investigation, she was sure.

They looked in all the rooms before returning at last to the hallway where Tarsh still stood on guard. Krasne had returned to sit beside the incinerated dust of Barces' remains. He had the firestick cradled in his arms and looked wary and unhappy. Taraganam was now inspecting the small room with the metal door where Parlòp had found the empty casket.

The final doorway off the hall, further along the wall, led to a long narrow room. There were no cupboards or cabinets in there. Again much of what must have been its furniture had decayed and deteriorated, collapsing into untidy debris. At the farthest point of the room, Parlòp found two dark wooden staffs leaning against a wall, surrounded by destruction. How could they be wooden and have survived the hundreds of years since the ravaging? She took one of them in her hands. She liked the smoothed knottiness of its feel. It felt, for a moment, almost warm to the touch. She felt a comfort, holding it in her hands. She looked at the other staff but arbitrarily kept the one she had taken first. It was the nicest one.

She turned it in her hands. It looked and felt like wood. She lifted it. It had a strong feel to it. It gave her confidence, something she had not realised was missing. It was a staff for the world of the plant and the animal. The world in which she dwelt, the world to which she ached to return. The stave made her feel more positive about being trapped in this endless labyrinth of stone and metal. It reminded her of her swamp and her wooden temple of grown and guided trees, the world of reeds and swamp. It was a worthy staff for her to bear. With it, she knew she would return to her home. It was a good feeling. And a staff was always useful – if only for hitting people.

She walked back to the hall and paused. The scene before her was of devastation and madness. Scattered across the floor, none of the bestial forms remained alive. But a living Saimar still dozed in the middle of them. The carcass of the kinfar, smouldering, blocked the way back up. The blockage was complete. She knew it even if others doubted it. They could not go back. The arch would collapse more if they even managed to move the carcass. Burn it and the roof would still fall.

Tarsh was guarding the other archway. His sword was out. He did not look pleased. He had massacred all the strange half-animal-half-woman forms that had filled the space – but it had given him no peace.

Krasne had found a strange metallic cloth to lay over them over Barces. His hand was on the firestick. Was he about to do something with it? Or did he fear that something would come upon him? He sat, forlorn, as if unable to conceive of what to do next.

Taraganam was standing listlessly outside the smallest of the rooms, the one with the metal door. It was as if she could not summon up the energy to explore any more rooms. She had looked across as they emerged.

'So,' said Parlòp. 'Are we staying, or do we descend?'

'We cannot leave Barces!' Tarsh said sharply.

'I think it best to wait for the Kelsari to come.' It was Krasne from across the room. 'He will bring more men and can dig us out.'

'But there may be an exit below,' said Taraganam. 'And we must still pursue the killer of Kalanomena.'

'There is also the shadow apparition,' said Krasne, tiredly. 'It keeps ahead of us, but eventually, it will be cornered. I do not want more of us to die. We came here to discover why Kalanomena was murdered, not to engage with monsters and cause more death. We must await more strength. The Kelsari will come.'

Parlòp walked over to the arch where Tarsh stood, sword in hand. She looked through it and onto the landing. Stairs stretched downwards in the same way as before.

'We do not know he will be able to get through without collapsing the arch,' said Taraganam. 'To wait merely delays. Let us find out what lies beneath.'

Parlòp had the feeling once more that Taraganam's hidden goals, her secret knowledge, was playing a part in her words. She wondered again what it was.

She did not sense the shadow beast. It was not lurking just

below them. She could not see if there was, as before, another landing below without moving some way down the stairs. But if the wretched creature had been there, she would have felt it.

She turned back and gazed at them all.

'I say send a party to scout for dangers ahead,' she said. 'Krasne, you can stay. Set up a camp and wait.'

Chapter 7

'For the mystic, the path of life leads upward.'

From The Way of the Solp

Krasne rose slowly to his feet. He looked angry.

Strangely, she sensed Krasne was also resigned. He knew he would lose the argument. Parlòp grasped her staff a little harder. She felt fleetingly uncertain. This was a Kelsara officer she respected. His only motivation was for good. He wanted to be cautious. That was understandable. They were in a dangerous place. Their search for the murderer of Kalanomena had abruptly become a fight for survival. She gazed at Krasne standing aggressively, challenging them in the silence. Yet she felt he knew that everyone, apart from his own man, Tarsh, was in favour of continuing. But he was not convinced; it was etched on every feature of his face. Parlòp ran nervous fingers along the smooth surface of her staff. Its presence gave her strength.

'Very well,' Krasne said savagely. 'Tarsh, set up a camp here. Secure this area as a place we can use to retreat.'

Tarsh stepped forwards. 'I don't want to stay here alone.' He sounded resentful. But Parlòp knew his main drive was fear – worry of being forsaken and abandoned. Even here where he was surrounded by the slain, the senseless lustful things he had massacred. How did she know that?

'I don't want more unnecessary deaths,' said Krasne sharply, scowling at his man. 'These three fools want to move further on, some fantasy that to get out of this place we must go deeper. You stay here, safe, and await the Kelsari.'

'I would be alone!' said Tarsh sharply. 'And surrounded by this . . . If you leave I will follow . . .' He hesitated and then slowly said, 'sir.'

Krasne seemed to consider making it an order but, in the end, his grim look was replaced by surrender. 'Very well. You are all utterly stupid, but it is my role... our role to protect you. Go forward then. *"There's no hope at the bottom of an unfathomable torrent."* May the consequences fall upon you all.'

'It is not so foolish to go forward,' said Taraganam. 'Remember when we first descended there was a second set of stairs, going to the right. We went left. Perhaps they connect at the bottom. Then we can ascend again from the depths and appear at that junction. It could be circular.'

Krasne growled some incomprehensible words and strode across the chamber, torch in one hand, firestick in the other. He reached Parlòp and Tarsh at the exit and gestured harshly at Parlòp with the firestick.

'Go then,' he said. 'Tarsh and I will follow.' He was angry but resigned at the same time. It was strange to be so sure of his feelings.

Parlòp stroked the smoothness of the staff. She had not intended to antagonise the officer. He was one of the more sensible Kelsar. Krasne and herself were the only ones trying to be sensible – to simply do their jobs – Fount Caresma and Taraganam Karsara, less so.

But her job was, as always, to discover, to understand and to teach. For that, she needed to proceed. And not only that, but maybe to save the shadow beast. Yet, even with that goal foremost, she regretted that she had alienated this Kelsara. For a runneler, he was close to reasonable.

She glanced down at Saimar. He was resting on the ground beside her. He knew they were descending and had come to her, ready. The allarg had simple loyalty. That was why she summoned him as often as she did. He was not complex or anxious. He trusted her. It was admirable, the trust of an animal when they knew you. He held no complexity, no dissembling, no pretence. They were what they were – not like people.

And that was also the reason she must, somehow, save the shadow.

Banging her staff decisively on the ground, Parlòp hesitated no longer. She walked down the steps, holding her torch aloft. Saimar scuttled beside her, keeping up. She heard and felt Krasne and Tarsh, together, marching rigidly down the steps behind her. The two wize, Karsara and Kelsara came behind them.

In some strange way, she sensed them all, not only their presence but each individually. Normally, she could not sense people as well as animals. Her own mind, her feelings and thoughts got in the way of feeling other people. Like listening to music when there is another tune playing. Animals were easy in comparison because their consciousness, their being was different. But now, for some reason, sensing people was all a lot clearer than she had ever known. She rubbed her fingers down the staff as she walked and wondered.

Parlòp reached the next landing and, as before, the stairs turned before descending. And then, faintly at first, she smelt some terrible stench below. It was tangible in the air, a smell of corruption and decay. She hesitated a short time and then walked on down. The smell became stronger the further she descended. There was something deeply rotten below. She wondered if it was excrement she could smell, the spoor of some animal perhaps rather than anything else. But it was an almighty stench as they descended. She heard gasps of disgust from behind her. She was relieved that Krasne did not use the opportunity to repeat that they had been wrong to descend.

Parlòp walked more slowly, but she did not stop. She was reaching the second landing before she realised that it did not, this time, open onto the next hallway. The stairs turned again and continued down. She paused, feeling a little unsure of their intent to go even lower. Wherever they were heading it was very deep indeed. Was this going to be the bottom of these vaults? If so, perhaps they were close to the conclusion, close to understanding what was happening, what had happened. If these were truly the basements of this place they might indeed contain another route – up. Maybe they could flee this foul place. But then maybe whoever had killed Kalanomena could escape too. Perhaps this whole exercise had been pointless because the murderer had fled long ago and had just left these horrors and a miserable shadow beast afraid of itself, in fear for its life. And no one even believed it was a life worth saving – except her.

She carried on. No one questioned her about the momentary pause. Perhaps they all felt the same thing, a sudden clenching of the stomach, not only at the stench that filled the air but at the thought of what might lie ahead.

The stairs went down through another two landings. What had they wanted to bury so deep? She thought if this was a place of work, of investigation and trial, why could it not have been done in the city above? Why bury it so deep in the ground, far beneath the river in the rock. What had they feared?

The stink was still growing. It was so strong now that she thought she might vomit. But it was hours since she had eaten and if she had it would only have been a dry heaving. She managed to hold on to herself. The bile rose in her throat but she forced it back down, feeling the acid burn her throat.

As they turned on the final landing she could see the lowest floor. It was slick with some awful lumpy wetness. It was not simply water, not clear or dark with dirt. She saw colour and unevenness to the slime; it was a pile of something rotting. But what was it? She could not see.

Why were there rotting things here? They could not have survived since Vyderbo was deserted and destroyed. Why create such a thing? Why had whoever had done this created decay?

She was halfway down the final set of steps when she sensed

them. *There is life below.* They were not animals, not even like the strange half women figures they had destroyed above. They were not sentient, not even as much as the calm and cautious trees. This life, the creatures ahead were just a hunger, a desire to consume, to eat and eat and grow. To become, to develop, to change.

The sensing was powerful. She wondered at its strength. The only thing like it that she knew was in nematodes and invertebrates, intestinal and soil worms that lived and consumed their way through their lives, pausing only to reproduce.

Then she understood that what she could see at the bottom of the steps was rotting food. There must have been many of the worms below, feeding. She smelt the stink very clearly now.

'What is it?' said Krasne from behind. She heard an edge to his voice born, she knew, of his fears and his remaining anger in equal measure.

'Nothing,' she replied. She could not, as ever, reveal what she sensed. 'It just smells awful down here – like rotting food.'

Was that convincing enough?

'We can suffer it, or we can return,' he said. 'I care not.'

She glanced back at him. She still regretted the alienation of this man. She walked slowly forward, using the staff to support her descent. It was going to be disgusting down here, she could tell. But if they were to investigate further, if they were going to find another way out of this place, it was going to have to be faced.

There could surely not be any danger from such creatures as she sensed. Worms feeding on the rottenness, contributing to it. There would be just disgust and nausea. She sent a wordless order to Saimar not to eat the rotting food below. The last thing she needed now was a sick allarg. He growled a resentful but obedient understanding. She looked down at the allarg. It was strange. She sensed his feelings more powerfully than she ever had before. The understanding was so strong that she could have felt what it was to be behind his eyes, to be him.

She was a few steps from the bottom when she saw a writhing movement in the food. There were worms, maggots, infesting it. She felt a wave of revulsion. The rottenness of swamp slime was pleasant by comparison.

What was going on? First a shadow monster of a childhood nightmare, then images of lust and the creation of a savage and violent kinfar. Why now piles of rotting food? Why kill Kalanomena? They needed to understand. If Kalanomena and now his killer had found the means to create – to make the phantasms of the wize real and actual – why was he, or she, creating awfulness?

She stepped off the last step, her bare feet squelching into the disgusting mess that covered the bottom landing. She ignored her rising nausea and turned, raising her torch. Oh, to be in the swamp and pushing her feet down into clean mud.

Ahead was another large chamber as there had been above. The bile rose again in her throat, burning in her gullet. The floor of the chamber was awash with rotting food. Her torch, and the light from Krasne's and Tarsh's behind her, did not reveal the far side. But there was no reason to think the sea of decay ended before it reached it.

If the food had ever been fresh, it had been a feast beyond telling. Before her were the rotting remains of every dish of the Karsar and Kelsar that she knew – and many she did not. There were great haunches of meat, rotting on great golden platters, mounds of browned fruit and perishing vegetables – cooked and served in great bowls. Sweetmeats and desserts were mixed and decaying with Kelsar fish dishes and the roasted legs of the giant kinfar of the plains.

And it was all writhing and squirming with the worms and maggots that devoured it. The reeking stink of the decomposing feast was overpowering.

'It's revolting,' said Tarsh with feeling.

Parlòp glanced back at him. That was blindingly obvious.

'Do we cross?'

'We can't go back except to wait and hope,' said Taraganam. 'Let us find out whether there is a way forward before we give up. We must discover what is on the other side of this chamber.'

'If anything,' said Krasne, with some feeling.

Parlòp decided that they had to move – and swiftly before they all vomited. She could not have borne it if they had started a long discussion while surrounded by such a nauseating mess. She walked forward, kicking great piles of food out of her way. The allarg beside her followed, snapping and snarling and sliding through the rotten food. But he was obedient. She felt his feelings. He did not eat.

She moved, gross as it was to step through the piles of putrefaction and worm castings. As she moved out into the chamber she realised there were wide doorways on either side. It was similar to the rooms above. There was more to the complex beyond the hall. Yet as far as she could see in their torchlight, the food and decay continued beyond these wide entrances. No wonder there were worms and maggots. This feast was greater, more massive than any amount of food she had ever seen or imagined.

As they reached the centre, she dimly made out the further archway ahead of them. The stench was worse. The rotting piles contained what looked like animal excrement as well as food. She wondered briefly what was defecating here. Another horror? She must hurry.

She felt a great wave of a mindless craving sweep over her. The strength of it was staggering. Such was its power that she was penetrated with a sudden and overwhelming desire to throw herself to the ground and eat. Were all the worms and maggots, with one mind, rushing to eat? But that could not be. They did not work together. She contained herself, rubbing anxious fingers down the smoothness of her staff.

Then she sensed them. They were coming.

'No!' she screamed.

Huge soilworms burst through the doors on either side. They were immense, higher than a person, with wide and rapacious maws surrounded by great hooked mandibles. If their mouths grasped you, then you would be pulled in. They were simply and completely designed to consume. There was nothing else.

Saimar snarled. The worms sped across the floor, scattering food. He snapped at the one heading for him. It did not pause. Krasne shouted something incomprehensible and flame belched from the firestick in his hands.

Tarsh leapt behind his officer. He turned to face the three giant worms coming from the other direction, slashing desperately with his sword. He sliced a chunk out of the first, but the others reached him and engulfed him.

'Run!' screamed Caresma as fire belched around him, burning to a crisp the worm that attacked him.

How did he do that? Did Krasne—?

But Parlòp had no time. It was not far to the archway at the end of the chamber. She dashed forward through the muck, spraying it upwards in a great wave of nauseous putrefaction. Saimar snarled and snapped his way beside her. He leapt ahead of her grasping a great worm in his jaws and, snapping it in two, throwing the pieces aside. The two halves rose to renew their attack.

Parlòp ran to the doorway and without a pause ran through it, hoping beyond hope that the stairwell did not lead to more steps down, descending into more filth and degradation.

The stairs went up.

She sprinted up, Saimar at her heels. *This could be a way out.* Fire belched behind her, filling the stairwell with light. She dared not turn and look. She dashed up the stairs to the next landing, which turned and continued upwards. She risked a glance back.

They were behind her. Krasne was at the rear shooting some worms that were trying, with difficulty, to follow. Caresma was beside him. Somehow, the fire from Krasne's stick was fiercer and more powerful. Parlòp did not understand. Was the Fount projecting a phantasm of fire? But surely no worm had brains enough to be fooled by phantasy, let alone run from it. Did he have a means of creating fire? She sensed a mystery about this Kelsara. Parlòp shook the thoughts from her head. It was not a time to wonder. It was a time to do.

The whole of the stairwell was filled with fire and light. The worms that had tried to crawl after them were consumed in brightness and ferocity. Taraganam was one step below Parlòp, Krasne and Caresma on the landing itself. But . . .

'Where is Tarsh?' Parlòp screamed.

'They took him,' said Taraganam, her face working with desolation and disgust. 'Because they were consuming him, we had time to escape.'

Krasne swore at her, some incomprehensible word in the tongue common to Kelsar and Karsar. Taraganam knew what it meant. Her face reddened with anger and shame. Krasne stopped firing and the fire that had seemed to emanate from Caresma's hands ceased at the same moment. *It must have been a delusion.* Krasne stormed up the stairs to Taraganam. He swore again in their language.

'Do not touch me!' screamed Taraganam. 'I am the servant of Turganamena. He will not abide—'

Krasne ground to a stop, seemingly coming to his senses moments away from throwing Taraganam to the floor. He was a guard of the Kelsari. He must not attack the embassy of the greatest of the wize. It would be war. Parlòp understood.

'I told you someone would die if we went on.' He shouted the words directly into her face. His features were twisted and filled with anger but Parlòp knew it was from his fear and anguish that the rage came.

'I was not alone in wanting to move on,' she said, her voice calmer than her look of indignant affront.

'Yes,' said Caresma from beside Krasne. 'We all forced you, Krasne. We forced it. We are responsible for Tarsh's death. You were right. There was a danger of more death. There still is.' Krasne turned to glare at him, his features still working. But his composure was returning.

'We must continue,' said Caresma quietly. 'They could yet follow.'

'Yes,' said Taraganam.

'They will eat what is closest first,' said Parlòp gently. 'We disturbed their feeding. They attacked for fright as well as the desire to consume.' She paused. 'They have much to consume...'

Krasne was calmer but he turned to glare at Parlòp for a moment – her words offended him. He had a strangely confused look of incomprehension on his face now. The shock and fear had engulfed him. 'But we must go, yes.' His voice was almost back to some fragment of normal. 'And we must somehow block the way behind us.'

They all turned and looked at Parlòp – as if she was in charge and it was only by her leave they could move. She turned and mounted the stairs, swinging her staff upwards. Saimar waddled beside her, growling his upset.

She ascended. *What horrible thing will be next?* But she walked on. They climbed through two more landings. Then as she turned right on the one before the last, she saw ahead a bright light. The landing above should be the one that opened onto another chamber. And it was filled with a golden glow, which flickered like candlelight. Yet there was a strangeness to it, an unreality. It was no candle she had ever seen. It was too bright as well.

Ahead she felt the shadow beast. It was within the chamber

above and it wasn't happy. It was not afraid – no more than usual. It was upset with what surrounded it. Who, perhaps? What was ahead? Who was ahead? Had they found the murderer of Kalanomena or something else? She stopped. They all stopped behind her.

'What is it?' said Caresma.

Chapter 8

*'I was there,
When he established the skies,
when he drew a circle on the face of the deep,
when he made firm the stars above,
when he established the fountains of the deep.
I was there.'*

The Creation Song

'The light . . .' said Parlòp, indicating with her staff. 'What is it?'

'We won't find out by standing here,' said Caresma.

'She is being cautious,' said Krasne sharply. 'We could do with more or it.'

And he was right. She had been foolhardy. They all had – except him. Krasne knew it. She knew it. Their heedlessness was why Barces and Tarsh were dead. She and the others had pushed too hard, driven the party onwards for reasons of their own. She sighed and regret flooded her.

They all had reasons.

And Parlòp had – to rescue the shadow beast.

She stood still. The silence stretched out. As tranquillity enveloped her she realised that she really could discern the emotions of the people around her. She had only been able to do it well with animals before.

Yet the sensations within Saimar beside her were also stronger. Her connection to him was still the strongest. She knew Saimar's being utterly.

She grasped the staff. This increase had been developing ever since she had taken this staff for her own. It must have been responsible for her new-found insights. Did it magnify the reality around her? Did it vibrate somehow in common with life? A clear pool on a summer's day, reflecting the sunlight from itself?

Whatever the truth, she felt so self-possessed, so sure of her mystical skills with the staff in her hands. It was not simply a wooden staff. It was some device of the ancients. She was fortunate to have found it.

The party around her was nervous and scared. The words they spoke were not their thoughts, not their most profound feelings. Their speech was a mixture of fear and bravado. It was not their deep emotions. Their perceptions and ideas welled around her like the different strains of some strange song. Each of them was like an individual tune, the same tones with differing timbres, varying resonances. It was like she was surrounded by eerie music, a song that made all life up, a rhythm by which it was formed and held together. And like music when you concentrated, you could hear each instrument. Did the universe itself sing? Each particle vibrating in pitch with the other – yet each unique unto itself. Each stone, each rock vibrating its existence within the whole music.

She did not know how long she stood there, entranced by the music around her, the music of the party. Was it just a second or perhaps a lifetime?

No one bothered her. No one spoke.

Caresma was different, she realised. He did not feel like the others. He didn't even vibrate like the animals she knew so well, the people who surrounded him. He was strange. He had a different quality. His nature was chasmic. His music was not discordant, but it was alien as if it belonged to the larger tune, a wider melody.

He had a strange confidence, a surety in his capabilities and his superiority. It was confusing. Yet it was more than confidence. It was more than arrogance. He was supremely sure of his own . . . supremacy. His emotions were that he was part of the main theme of the song. All the others were secondary. Everything was secondary. They were accompaniments. He sang the only true melody. It was all of them who were discordant, they who were the lesser harmony. Why was that? Who was he? She knew she should find out what was deeply different about this Fount of the Kelsar wize. But when would she be able to do that? And how would she force him to tell her? It was too much. She could not solve Caresma easily. She had sensed this difference before. Perhaps the knowledge of it would be enough, to watch him, to be ready.

She must start moving again. Had not an age passed by? They would reprimand her in a moment. She must stop musing on the nature of the universe – of Caresma – and act. The others followed her. Had but a moment had gone by or a lifetime?

She walked up the stairs. She sent a calming understanding to the shadow beast she knew was ahead. All she got in response was a wave of unhappiness. Unlike the Fount, its emotions were clear. She sent a powerful beam of trust at the beast. She had never known she could cast with such power. It was urgent. It was key. She must save this creature.

Warily, they approached the landing. The golden light in the chamber ahead was very bright. It flickered, but brighter than many candles. She reached the top and turned to look through the archway to the chamber beyond.

The hall ahead was piled with treasures. Immense heaps glinted and glowed in the strange golden light. She could not quite believe what she saw. Around her were mountains of gold and gemstones. She could see some of the sea-gems that river people gathered from molluscs along the coast. But there was so much of it. Parlòp had never seen such a fortune. The floor of the great hall was filled with a fortune beyond counting. Precious metals, coins, gems and jewellery were spread over the place in huge piles.

She looked up. The flickering golden light came from tall plinths with what looked like flames dancing atop them. She saw no people, but she felt the shadow beast. There was more than this. There were again doorways on both sides of the hallway. The beast was hiding somewhere in this complex of rooms.

She stepped forward, unsure.

What danger would there be here?

'Amazing,' said Caresma from behind her. 'Such riches.'

Strangely, no desire for wealth was held in his voice. The treasure left him completely unaffected. He did not mean the words.

'We won't be short of money for a while,' he said.

It was an attempt at hilarity and an attempt to say, to be what he should be. He was acting. He was playing at being Fount of the Kelsar wize. It was not his real self. That was elsewhere.

Parlòp's attention returned to the riches before her. Solving Caresma must wait. Whoever was doing all this was creating things he or she desired – lust, anger, food and now money. What would come next? Power?

But whoever they were, they had that in abundance. Wasn't the power to create these dreadful visions enough for anyone? Yet, this fulfilment of all their desires was another form of misery – these piles of wealth, another nightmare.

Who would die here? Someone always died.

She walked forward into the brightness.

She felt Krasne grasping her from behind. 'Be careful,' he said and stepped quickly forward to stand beside her. Saimar, scuttling out of his way, resented him taking his favoured position. She felt his resentment flowing out, much stronger than she had ever had an understanding from him.

She voiced him a calm and looked down at the allarg. His resentment was no more than mild displeasure at being usurped. Such had been the strength of her understanding that it had confused her. She stroked the staff in her hand. This would take getting used to, and the magnification of her ability was increasing.

She saw no one in the room. It looked safe.

The whole area was visible in the brightness of the plinth. Parlòp doused her torch. It would be best to save its fire – the torches would not last forever. She heard the others following her lead and dousing their torches. Such was the brightness that the light around them was not dimmed.

Was it time to summon the shadow beast? If the staff enhanced her powers, her sensitivity, her understanding, wouldn't it accentuate the other gifts of life-magic given to the Solpsar by the Great Maven Franeus? She could calm the shadow. She would save the beast. If it was next to her she could overcome the fears that filled it with a discordant clangour.

She kicked the nearest pile of gems out of the way. They slithered noisily to the floor in a rushing, scraping slide.

'Be silent,' said Krasne and swore, a runneler obscenity. He paused. 'There will be some new terror awaiting us here. Trust me. This venture is cursed.'

'But it is so quiet,' said Taraganam from behind in the archway. 'Perhaps there is nothing here, no one – just wealth.'

'The shadow beast is here,' said Parlòp before she could stop herself.

Krasne glanced at her and walked abruptly into the room. 'Where?' He raised the firestick.

She stepped hastily forward and grabbed his arm. 'No. It's not going to attack. It is frightened. I can call it. I can subdue the dread. It will come to me. It will not attack.'

Krasne looked at her. 'I know you swampers are good with beasts. Surely this one is beyond your ability to tame.'

Parlòp knew that regardless of the risk of exposure, she had to be clear with this Kelsara guard. 'I can do this,' she said urgently. She glanced back. 'I would have done it in the first corridor if Taraganam had not arrived and interrupted. It is frightened. Do not scare it more. Any cornered beast will fight.'

Krasne looked at her for a long, heart-stopping moment. 'Go at it, swamper.' He paused and lifted the firestick. 'I'll be ready when it kills you.'

Yet Parlòp knew he had a grudging respect for her. She did for him. He didn't think she would die. He thought she would succeed. His dignity just would not allow him to say it.

'Keep the wize from following,' she said, without looking back at them.

Through the doorways, in the rooms on either side, were yet more piles of riches. She could not imagine how much this would be valued by the Kelsar when they realised it sat in the vaults. The merchants from the southern and western lands would be very busy trading for many years to come. It would establish the wealth and power of the river people for centuries.

It was not a good thought.

She hefted her staff and tried to sense in which direction the beast was. It was to her left. She felt it, far through the middle of the three doors on that side. She glanced to the right. There were four doors on the other side. It was not there.

She looked down at Saimar and decided the beast would be scared of him. She ordered him to remain with Krasne.

He growled at her fiercely. He did not agree. Such was the force of the understanding, she was almost overwhelmed by the strength of his emotion. She calmed herself. She ordered him again, powerfully, and the growl lessened until he was just grumbling to himself. She walked away.

Holding the staff held across her chest like a baton, she walked towards the doorway, kicking aside piles of jewellery and gems to reach it.

Light streamed through the doorway. There must be another of the glowing golden plinths inside. She reached the entrance to a large room beyond, containing more piles of riches. But it had no furniture in it, or at least none that had survived the centuries as the metal drawers and cabinets had in the higher rooms. The plinth with its flickering golden light stood in the centre of the room.

Feeling the gaze of the three behind her, who were no doubt wondering what she was looking at, she stepped forward. She stopped.

A man sat with his back to the plinth, facing away from her. She could only see his arm along the side. Well, it looked like a man's arm. He wore a robe. Why had she not sensed him? He didn't move. Was he dead? They had hardly been silent during their arrival in the outer hall. If he was listening then he would surely have heard them and reacted – if he could. *He must be dead.* But she did not move.

She could not see the shadow beast. It was further in. There were more doorways at the end of the room leading, no doubt, to another complex of corridors as on the other floors. She stood silent. Should she proceed? Was the man alive or dead?

She turned and indicated the Krasne to come to her. She motioned to him to be quiet. He nodded and, before moving, turned around and glared at the two wize. He wanted them to stay where they were. But as he moved carefully across the hall they quietly trailed after him. He did not remonstrate with them.

Like her, he was resigned to their idiocy. They would not obey an order from either of them. They would not listen because what Parlòp had discovered might give them what they wanted.

Krasne reached her. Parlòp silently indicated the arm of the man beside the plinth. Krasne turned and scowled at the wize behind. She was unsure why, for in the next breath he challenged the man loudly.

'Whoever you are, we come in peace. Are you . . .?' He stopped because the arm moved and the man spoke.

'Be silent. You are mine. I made you. I can unmake too. I don't remember, but . . .' He paused as if speaking was a nuisance. 'Go away. I can annihilate you. There is nothing I cannot do. Everything is mine.'

'Kalanomena,' Taraganam shouted. 'Is that you? How can it . . .?'

The voice spoke again. 'Tara, I made you – too many of you. It got out of hand in my head. You were always . . .' He hesitated. 'Go away. Go and play with the others.'

Taraganam ran. Could it be that she had cared for him as much as he had lusted for her? She swept by them – Krasne tried to grab her. He tripped over a pile of jewellery and was on his feet in a moment, but she was past. Taraganam stopped and stared down at the man still sitting, his back against the plinth.

'How can it be you? It is you. But you are dead. You were dead. We cremated your body.' She shook her head as if shaking off a dream. 'I was there . . .'

'Go away,' said Kalanomena. 'You are a phantasm. I don't want to play anymore . . . even if it was fun a while.' He looked up at her. 'What is truth anyway? It's an elusive thing – and adrift in a sea of imagining. Is it important what is real and what I make? Maybe they are the same. Is there anything concrete? And everything is just my . . .'

'You don't you think it's me?' she said. 'Do you think I am one of the vile forms that you made? We destroyed them all.'

'I know that I made you . . . I can make everything . . .' said Kalanomena. Was there a moment's lucidity? Then, shaking his head, he returned to his chaos of unknowing – muttering nonsense and doubts in a moment's breath. His was a song descending into cacophony.

Krasne moved forward. But before he got a step, Caresma strode purposefully past him. Krasne made another ineffectual attempt to stop him. But he did not look like he cared that much.

Parlòp took a step back. She looked down at Saimar who was lying beside her, uninterested in their argument. She crouched next to him and ran her fingers over his gnarly back.

'You conjured yourself – you fool!' said Caresma. 'Your ka is fractured. Unify yourself!'

'I know I made me. But he wasn't me. I'm me,' said Kalanomena. 'He was but the shadow. I am the best. I was the knowing one. He was my weakness. He was unaware, unmindful of the power. He was lost in his darkness and doubt. He had to be destroyed.'

'You killed your shadow-ka?' Taraganam looked shocked at her own words. 'You murdered yourself.'

'That is not how minds work,' Caresma declared. 'As a wize, you know this. You ... we need both darkness and light in the mind – the shadow-ka and the pach-ka. They cannot be separated. The ka is one. The shadow gives birth to good as well as to bad. The light in us can create evil too.' He paused. 'Surely you remember.'

Imperiously, Kalanomena rose to his feet.

Parlòp saw the whole of him – a flaxen-haired man dressed in the robes of a Karsara wize. He held a crystal loosely in his right hand, which glowed with an inner fire. But it flickered with blackness and white together, a never-ending dance around each other. It was not large, only the size of the tapple fruit.

Kalanomena glared. 'I am beyond such infantile understanding, apparition of Caresma. Begone, you phantasms. I will undo you.' He brandished the gem. 'You are not here. You are an illusion. Everything is. I can make life. I can destroy it too. I am life and I am death. There is nothing to be but what I decree.'

After this, they used too many jargon words and Parlòp could not follow. Their argument became very technical. She had never had any interest in the abstruse magic of the wize. Wisdom, they said, but only used for evil and domination. But she was not interested in such ideas, mystic though she was. She was of the swamp and life itself was all the magic she wished to understand or to surround herself with. Life itself was the only true wisdom, to bend yourself to it and to take its insights into your being. This was all that was important.

The wize lived their whole lives creating that which was not. She only valued what was outside herself and the understanding it brought within. The wize only valued what was inside their minds, and entirely of themselves.

She lifted the staff. It was true. It reverberated with the song of life. She vibrated with its being. The staff was the source of the deepening of her power, the growing strength of her connection with the rhythm of life around her. *No, it is not the source.* The magic was not in the staff. It was not even in her. They both simply trembled in mutuality with something underneath. There was a song in reality. Everything vibrated with an individual tone, its own timbre. The music it made was existence. The staff and she were in resonance with the true song.

She reached out to the shadow beast. It was further into the chambers beyond. She could understand it now, stronger than she had ever done.

It did not like Kalanomena, the Karsara who had given it birth. It feared him. His fear was the depth of its being. It was afraid of him and for him. It had liked the shadow-ka part of him that he had killed. It had tried to save him.

Parlòp understood then.

This Kalanomena was the shadow copy. This Kalanomena had killed his true self. And the beast . . . the beast had saved the fractured ka of Kalanomena. The beast had carried his body to the surface. It had run, pursued by this broken piece of him. He had wielded the firestick. He had pursued them, trying to annihilate. And it had carried him, dead though he was. It had gone up all the landings and stairs until it even carried him outside.

Until the beast's fears of the world overcame it. The outlandish outside was, in the end, more frightening than the dangerous phantasies of the vault. And it had dropped him in the square and hurried back to known places. It had lived its whole existence there. Even though it contained the shadow Kalanomena, it was its home . . .

She sent calmness through the understanding and she felt the rhythm of the beast's fear change. She summoned the beast and felt it move, coming to her. Anxious but desirous of standing with her, of linking itself to her.

Parlòp crossed to the far side of the room. The four of them were still talking as she passed. Their voices rose and fell as one after another they expressed their anger.

The beast emerged from a broken doorway, its blackness and its ferocity undimmed. Yet there was the possibility of it not being afraid – of having a friend who would stand with it. A friend who might make the world less weird and unknowable. The beast came right up to her and she reached out a hand and touched the claws – vile, ferocious claws imagined by the child Kalanomena. The beast bowed its head as if in relief. She stroked its impossible maw. She turned to return to the others and Kalanomena – if that was who he truly was.

As she turned the Karsara, the insane one, strode towards her. But he spoke to the shadow beast. 'So, you return, do you, the phantasm of a child – the foolish defender of the lost one? Shall I unmake you now?' He stopped and peered strangely at Parlòp. 'When did I make a swamper?'

She saw again lucidity in his eyes, a doubt in the certainties of derangement. Then the moment was gone and he sniggered. 'What was the point in that? What was the point of the swamp? Mind you, she is quite nice to look at.' He guffawed quietly to himself.

Taraganam spoke, reaching out with her hand to Kalanomena's shoulder. 'We are real, Kala. It is truly us.' But something made her stop before the hand touched.

Caresma was peeved. 'We are real, Kalanomena Karsara. We

came to find who had killed you. We found where you broke through to these vaults.'

Kalanomena shook his head. He had turned but he was not looking at Caresma. He was gazing at Taraganam. 'No, foolish dreams. Tara, my love, there is only the reality I conjure. Now I can have you. You are no longer unobtainable. You are all figments of my power and skill. Perhaps there is nothing I cannot do or be with this...' He lifted the strange gem, the light in it dancing with light and shadow. 'Perhaps there was never anything but me. Perhaps you were all but a dream.'

Parlòp was relieved for the moment had passed. He had moved on, distracted by his madness She had feared that he would use the flickering gem on the shadow beast, uncreating it. *No, it deserves life.*

'Your sui is obliterated,' said Caresma. 'You need help, Kalanomena. We are the real. All this is but coalesced eidetic phantasms of your fractured ka. Reality hasn't changed. That is just some sort of energy source. You use it to synthesize matter, driven by your thaumatic magic. It has no meaning. Perhaps you are the copy. Maybe you murdered the real Kalanomena for the phantasies you see.'

Kalanomena laughed. It was not a normal laugh, not a joyous thing, not born of life and laughter. It was a broken laugh, the laugh of a person whose laughter has long turned to dust.

He glared at the Fount. 'You are real, are you, Caresma of the weak-willed Kelsar?' He giggled again, the nasty sniggering chortle. 'What of this then? Do you want some more reality? Is this real?'

Then, like the ripples of a clear pool when a rock is dropped in it, as when an allarg slips silently into the water to take its prey, the chamber around them wavered and was gone.

Chapter 9

'We are a part of the whole, limited.
We experience thoughts and feelings
as something separate,
the delusion of awareness.
This is a prison,
restricting us to ourselves and to the few.
Our goal must be to free our sentience
from this prison
by widening our compassion to embrace
all of life,
and the universe in its magnificence.'

After Aeisen, a teaching of the ancients.

Actuality coalesced.

She did not recognise where she was. It was no place of river or swamp that she had ever seen. They stood in the centre of a great palisade. Huge trunks of trees formed a paling fence curving between four huge stone towers. It formed a great circle around an enormous high single tower in the centre. At the top of this main tower was a crystal dome.

The wize could create a phantasy in your head that you were somewhere other than you really were. You were still just where you were before, but your mind could not comprehend that. You could not, without much skill, move the hand that you could no longer see or feel.

Parlòp had experienced these projected phantasies of the wize before. There were often skirmishes and outright battles between the swamp and the river. Her Solpsari, Fleráp's father, had died in a battle between beasts of the swamp and the phantasies of the river.

Was this what had appeared around her?

The shock of the transition drained from her and Parlòp realised what it must be. It was one of the Karsar towers. She had never seen one. They had been described but she had ignored the description. She'd had no intention of leaving her swamp. Kel'Katoh was alien enough for her, so to know what a Karsar tower was like was unnecessary.

But was this a phantasy or a solid phantasm like in the vaults? Had he created a whole tower and a whole place to put it in? Or could Kalanomena have transported them there – in reality? It looked awfully real.

People from the high tower were reacting. The sudden appearance of three wize, an allarg, a shadow beast, a swamper and a Kelsar guard in their midst would be provoking. The shock put paid to any niceties. Warriors were running towards them. They were coming from every area of the stockaded township, drawing, seizing and brandishing weapons – spears, great pikes, hammers, swords and axes. It did not look like a welcome.

Parlòp swung around, pulled the staff tight to herself and summoned both creatures. The shadow beast was already beside her, cowering. As her order reached its mind, it moved even closer, scuttling to be as near to her as it could. Its head was low and fear emanated from every pore of its being. Saimar scrambled to stand in front of her, his teeth-filled jaw towards the oncoming warriors. His tail lashed from side to side between her legs, and his defiant snarls filled the air. When the warriors attacked, Parlòp would have difficulty controlling him. The nature of a beast was always its essence.

The warriors were all around and they did not challenge. They hardly paused but for a momentary hesitation of preparation. Spears were thrown. Two, ill-thrown in panic, bounced off Saimar's gnarled skin. He snarled and snatched another from the air, breaking the shaft in two. The next spear hit him in his side, where the armour of his skin was a little weaker. It pierced him and he wailed a howl of pain and anger, snarled a vicious challenge back and lunged at the nearest soldier. The warrior wrenched a bloody leg from Saimar's maw before it closed. The allarg let him go.

More spears streaked through the air. Parlòp stepped forward, her legs straddling the allarg. She smashed two spears from the air with a swing of her staff. One more bounced from Saimar's scales and another, striking true, pierced his back.

'Cease at once!' Taraganam shouted. 'Stop. It is us.'

Parlòp saw but a brief pause. Did they recognise her? Did they know her voice? Were they really at one of the towers? Had Kalanomena somehow transported them?

As Taraganam's words echoed around, Kalanomena, beside her, gabbled a madman's wordless crazed challenge. Giant barqs burst into being beside him. They were huge with massive axes – their forms a nightmare. They were ghastly, covered in scale plates. Their faces were dreadful. Parlòp saw hesitation. Their axes swung. Many warriors of the tower perished before the blows – sliced in two, smashed and broken like the dolls of a violent child

Parlòp was horrified. They were real! But barqs were a myth, the monstrous fighters of children's fables. A legend had come to life.

Their massive blades rose again.

'Die, you fools,' Kalanomena screamed. 'I have returned. I claim dominion. This tower is mine. I have found the device of the legends. I am the creator. I make all. Existence is mine to ordain.'

The monstrous barqs strode out, continuing the attack, beating the warriors back with ferocious blows. Blood and gore spurted out and the warriors retreated, screaming, calling for aid. Parlòp dropped to her knees and pulled out the two spears that had pierced Saimar's side. Blood poured from the wounds. She glanced up, worried that she might be attacked.

The scene before her was confused. She was surrounded by a

vicious battle. Great reptilian winged creatures had appeared, the like of which Parlòp had never seen. They were terrible, some fervid creation of a night terror perhaps. Or were they an echo of the great chaos in the myths of the first day – the Dragon himself? Without a pause, the reptiles joined the attack with the barqs.

Ordering her two creatures, she rose, backing away as she did. The shadow beast was mauling a tower warrior who had tried to attack from the side. Its maw closed about his shoulder and the terrible claws raked him. He fell, screaming, blood pouring from gashed wounds. The beast turned and ran to her. Saimar was more reluctant to come. The threat, the pain of the attack had driven him into a fighting frenzy. Parlòp retreated hastily, summoning the allarg to her. She glanced backwards.

Behind her was the central tower. She did care. It was away from Kalanomena, away the source of the monsters filling the palisade. There were fewer warriors that way. Could she hide in the tower?

Krasne was beside her. She didn't know when he'd arrived. His firestick was blazing with light. Warriors who dared to prevent their retreat burst into flames and collapsed backwards in screaming death. But few attempted it. The barqs and the winged reptiles were killing too many.

Parlòp couldn't see Caresma or Taraganam. But she could hear Kalanomena's challenges. He was shouting in the Karsar tongue, his crazy screams echoing from the surrounding palisade wall. Parlòp voiced her creatures. They pelted backwards. Saimar snarled his defiance but the attacks on him of the tower warriors had abated. The shadow beast, bent low to the ground, lolloped beside her, next to Krasne. Its mind was filled with fear and sorrow. Did it regret coming with her? Would it have been safer in the vaults than this? If it did, it did not reproach her for her summons.

She would not blame it.

Parlòp reached the steps up to the tower entrance. Krasne was still beside her, the shadow beast on her other side. Saimar was in front, now fighting two warriors who had attacked from the left. They were intent on killing the allarg, to remove at least one threat from their tower. They were giving her, as a swamper, dark and violent glares. Did they think she was somehow responsible for it all? Krasne, from beside her, shot the firestick twice in quick succession and the two warriors burst into flames. Saimar scuttled back, treading over Parlòp's feet, snarling defiance, avoiding the flames.

Men came behind them, appearing from the tower doors. Parlòp swung around, lifting the staff as a weapon, assuming another attack. Two were robed as wize. The third, on the right, was a warrior with many daggers sheathed in his cuirass. The wize on the left cast quickly into the air.

More beasts, more warriors leapt into existence around them. A wall of fire burst into being around the tower, beyond Parlòp and Krasne. They would be phantasms. But they would confuse. No one would know the truth from the false. Reality and the imagined were lost in confusion.

The tallest of the robed wize, in the centre, was grey-haired. He stood, impassive. Parlòp stopped. What would these Karsar do? Did they believe they were fighting an attack of a rival wize merely casting disruptive phantasies? Surely they couldn't understand that Kalanomena was creating real phantasms. Then, as she watched, the grey-haired wize raised his hand and the world wavered and changed . . . again.

Parlòp despaired.

◊◊◊

They were surrounded by whiteness. The cold snatched her breath from her lungs. The chill air swept in and a brisk wind streamed across the ground towards them, kicking up the snowdrifts into whirlwinds of white. The cold passed through Parlòp's shift as if it were not there. Even the unguent of nargon sap on her skin did not stop the blast of iciness. Rawness penetrated to her very bones.

A massive snowscape stretched out from them – a harsh land of broken ice and snow. She swung round. The sun was turning to the afternoon, to the west. Far to their north were grim and forbidding white mountains streaked with grey. To the east was an icy and menacing stretch of a frozen sea. In the west, redness tinged the horizon as if a crimson sun was setting there, but the white glaring sun was above, chasing the red into the night.

Were these the ice-lands of the far north? Was this true or imagined? Confusion and doubt crept through her. She felt fear almost as a physical thing. How would they ever get out of this?

All who had been in the tower were there but far separated. Now it was easy to see everyone and who they were. The allarg and the shadow were many feet from her in front. Krasne was equally far off to her right. His firestick was a curved metal spoon. The warriors around them were all holding flowers, yellow and brown, like the sun on a beautiful day. Parlòp looked at her own hands. The staff she had been holding was just a broken, rotting piece of wood torn from some dead branch.

The monsters that Kalanomena had conjured still fought things she could not see. It was as if the images around them had no meaning for them. They were hitting no one, or so it appeared, for there was no one close to them.

'Fool, Turganamena!' screamed Kalanomena. 'My power is beyond this foolish image. I can create real worlds now. You cannot stand against me.'

'Stop, Kala! He is our lord,' Taraganam shouted. She was ten or so feet from him but moved, running towards him – a man for whom she cared.

'I have no lord. I am the maker,' cried Kalanomena and cackled his mad glee. He raised his fist which, it seemed, contained now only a piece of rock. Parlòp blenched. What now?

'You are a treacherous rebel,' Turganamena said quite calmly. 'Now you die.'

◊◊◊

The world wavered and they were back in the tower. Had they not left? It was all ridiculous. Turganamena was standing just behind her. Parlòp considered him, expecting some terrible attack.

Turganamena raised his hand. He did not speak. The warrior next to him wavered like the ripples of water in a swamp pool and disappeared. He had removed him from their perceptions – a mind-trick of the wize, but a useful one. He was invisible.

Parlòp looked forward. The world around her was in chaos – the fighting had resumed as if it had never paused. Krasne's firestick flashed beside her. Saimar was snarling and snapping at three warriors who were stabbing him with spears.

'Stop!' she shouted. She stepped forward to help the allarg, swinging her staff like a long cudgel and broke the heads of two of the warriors with one mighty blow. They fell. Parlòp swung her staff upwards again, cracking it into the shoulder of the third of the towerguards. The man screamed in pain and collapsed. Parlòp dived to the ground to the side of the allarg. Blood was pouring now from multiple wounds in his side and one great gash between his eyes. Only the toughness of his skin had prevented that blow from entering his skull and piercing the brain.

Parlòp summoned the beast and ordered it to defend. She bent down over the allarg as the blackness of the shadow beast enveloped her. She heard and felt its claws striking. It growled and snarled its distress and its defiance. It was released to its anger and its fear – a cornered animal.

Parlòp tried to staunch the blood streaming from Saimar's side. She tore her shift apart to make rags to press into the wound, to hold the blood. She hoped vainly that she could bandage his wounds, halt the draining life. But the blood was too fast. She burst into tears. They fell like rain onto the allarg's back. Saimar turned slightly, weakly, and looked up at her with shielded eyes. Parlòp saw only a strange alien, beastly look of resignation mixed with incomprehension in his eyes. Through the understanding she felt, deep within his being, fear and doubt streaming to her.

She could not save him.

The light went out in the allarg's eyes. His emotions collapsed around her like the crashing death of many trees on the day of a storm. She thrust up with her legs, moving, her back thudding against the body of the shadow beast that enveloped her.

She screamed a wordless curse of anger. They had killed Saimar.

She struck out, swinging the staff outwards in a great curve. There was no one in range for her to strike down. The beast had scared them. Its claws, either side of her, were dripping with blood. Above her, its teeth dripped with some fleshy gore. Parlòp tensed to leap forward, staff swinging, with the shadow beast at her side.

An ear-splitting scream cut suddenly off into a gurgle of death. At once Parlòp heard a second scream, a woman – the cry of distress and crushed love. Parlòp stopped. She looked.

Kalanomena was standing in the centre of the palisade, the gem slipping from his loosened fingers. A long thin dagger protruded from his neck. It had been plunged in one side and extended out of the other. Taraganam caught him as he staggered and fell. She grabbed him and let him slowly fall to the ground in her arms.

The assassin wavered into existence beside them. Behind her, Turganamena spoke. 'So die all traitors. I have my vengeance.' His words were deceptively calm.

Taraganam took the gem from Kalanomena's fingers. She turned and, with a look of pure hatred, she raised it. And the world was remade.

Chapter 10

'The brave way is to care for all life.'

The teachings of the Grand Mystic.

White and blazingly bright in the clear air, the sun was slipping behind the far mountains of a strange, ruined landscape. It was eerie. Silent. All the noise and ferocity of the battle in the tower had gone. The stillness rushed in and snatched the fear and anger away from her. Parlòp stared sightlessly at the world around her. She did not care where she was. The threat was gone.

Unthinking, she called the creatures to herself. The shadow was already above her and at her summons it collapsed backwards, hiding behind her back, retreating into bewilderment and fear.

Saimar did not answer. He was dead.

She bent over his body and cried. He would not come to her again. She would never again hear his answering snarl as she summoned him. She would never again sit on the bank near her temple and watch him cruising the river – his whole body except his eyes hidden below the water.

She cursed. Bitter tears flowed down her cheeks. She regretted ever calling him from his life in the swamp. He would be alive, hunting and content within his existence.

If I'd gone to the floating city alone . . . If I hadn't brought him to protect me against . . . the foul wiles of the runnelers.

At this wave of emotion within her, the shadow, on the ground behind her, lifted a gentle claw and ran it down her back.

It was still there. It would protect her. It would stay. The understanding flowed from it to her. She turned to gaze at it and it looked up at her. Its expression was unreadable, but she knew its feelings through the staff cradled across her lap. The beast had been scared of the allarg. Saimar, she knew, had not trusted the shadow. Within the rhythms revealed by the staff, their notes were discordant. Yet she, with it in her hands, could harmonise their differences and reveal a new tune. Now there was only the darkness of the shadow beast's emotions.

She leaned forward and stretched herself out on the back of the dead allarg, oblivious to his blood mixing with the green of the nargon unguent.

'He is dead then . . .'

She raised herself at the sound of the voice.

Krasne was beside her. 'The allarg perished . . .' He sounded like he cared. Perhaps he did. She stared at him, unable to process her feelings. She regretted the tactless responses to the deaths of Barces and Tarsh. Krasne had known them both in a way she had not. His emotion had been reasonable. She had been unfeeling. She knew that.

She looked beyond him and realised that they were all there – all five of them. The Kelsar guard was beside her. Beyond him, Taraganam was bent over the body of her love, Kalanomena. He too was dead, lost in his madness and slain by his lord. Taraganam was crying.

But Parlòp saw the shimmering shadow crystal held tight in her right hand. Her knuckles were white. Caresma was standing next to her. He looked like a man that wanted to do something but had no idea what it should be. As she watched, he raised his hands as if to touch Taraganam's shoulder and then let them fall to his side. He raised them again but still could not do it.

Parlòp turned back to Krasne. He was next to her but had fallen to his knees. He was gazing at her.

She spoke. 'The spears . . . there were too many. They killed him.' She felt the tears well up again as thoughts of Saimar's death were replayed in her head. This time she managed to stop herself crying.

Krasne shook his head. 'I have never trusted the wize, be they

Kelsar or Karsar. None of the riverguard do. To create that which is not real holds no interest. They play warfare through it. Only the real death of my men matters to me – Barces and Tarsh. I wish I had never come, never obeyed my king. I wish I was at home with my woman and my child.' He swallowed. 'We none of us will survive this, I think. We are lost in madness.'

Parlòp did not know how to respond. His words were undeniable. Krasne gave a slow resigned nod.

She turned from him and looked at the landscape around them. It was a bizarre place. The terrain was not normal. They were on a flat piece of ground but surrounding them were what would have been rolling hills of a pleasant country. But the hills looked as if they had melted as if blasted by some terrible heat – a land that had congealed and solidified. It looked like a pool of tallow wax, melted by some cruel and senseless child. Far to the west, the mountains were blackened and dark – burnt in some great fire. In the encroaching dusk, the hills in the far distance glowed with an ethereal green-blue light – a cold fire that never flickered. She had never seen anything like it. Where was she?

She turned and looked south to see a jagged edge that looked like it might once have been a building. It was whitened like ash, scorched then melted – like a strange broken toy thrown into the fire and turned to ash. Perhaps it was just a jumble of strange windswept rocks. Where were they? Was it real?

Krasne was talking. 'Lord Fount, is this the stone wilderness – the Har Kolem?'

'Yes, it is,' said the wize. 'And we are really here. It is no phantasm.'

How did he know that? The rest of them no longer knew what was real and what was imagined. Was there any difference?

'The tower of Turganamena was real too?' said Krasne.

The Kelsar wize nodded but did not speak.

Taraganam screamed some angry words in the Karsar tongue.

Parlòp did not know their language well, even though it was a dialect of Kelsar. But it was clear they were words of anger and bereavement, words of pain and anger. They were not directed at Krasne. They were words of grief.

Parlòp gazed at the wize woman, sobbing over the dead body of her man. She wondered if they had ever declared their attraction, their fondness for each other. Had Kalanomena dreamed his lustful dreams undeclared? And had she felt a strong attraction without ever speaking of it?

Parlòp could have tried to puzzle the meaning of her words out but somehow she could not summon the energy. The dead allarg was at her feet and, for her, that was more serious. The allarg had not deserved death. Perhaps Kalanomena had, despite Taraganam's feelings. His ambitions and obsessions were the cause of all of this. He had inflicted so much suffering and death.

The sun had reached the horizon. Indeed, its disc was half below it. Darkness was creeping into being around them. Was this then the Har Kolem – the stone desert? A quiver of fear ran down her back at the thought that they could have been transported to such a place. It was a poisoned land.

She knew little of it and wished to know less than she did. It was far to the south, beyond the Karsar lands. It was not a place of life; it was a place of death. No one crossed it. Those who had tried had often been taken sick afterwards. None of them, according to legends, ever survived. The ravaging had destroyed everything there, leaving only the poison – in the air and the rocks themselves. The myths said it had been a good land once, before the ravaging. The makkuz, the Hraddas, came from the stars and destroyed the civilization of the ancients. The cities that had been there crumbled and melted before the ferocity of their hatred. That was what she was seeing.

Beings of fire and heat, the makkuz had yet been able to appear as people. They had been hidden, watchers, but at the last, they had shown themselves and destroyed the great empire of the magician kings – and their servants, the Noble Warrior and the Great Maven.

Parlòp reached out and called the shadow creature to her. It came within her embrace. She wondered if they would all die now – poisoned by the land around them. She pulled the staff tight to her chest and wondered about running away. But she didn't. Who knew whether she might be poisoned more by running than by staying? Which was more dangerous – probable death or possible death?

The darkness was deep now. She had not seen any trees or wood they could have used to light a fire in the dark. They were doomed to a night in unbroken darkness.

'Can any of you cast light, or just the phantasy of one?' she said.

Krasne spoke from the darkness. 'There is no wood to light a fire.'

She hunkered down on the body of Saimar, with the shadow beast as a cloak about her. She pulled the staff to her and let it speak to her. Let the mind and feelings of the beast merge with her own. She projected calmness to the beast but did not feel it herself.

She gave herself to the song of the staff. With its power she let her mind move outwards. She felt it then; deep in the desert itself there was a strange impression. It was life, like an echo on a clear day or a whisper in a dark night. She felt the rhythms of faint emotion resonating through the staff – like the presence of a lover sleeping in the night. Was it some sort of memory? A remembrance of the thousands, millions perhaps, who had died there when the monsters from the sky had come. Were the myths true? She hugged the staff and tried, as best she could, to let the feeling that there had been life here once sweep through her. Was the memory of its greatness still there?

Darkness was deep around them. She could not see Krasne

beside her. The only light was the faint bluish-green glow over the distant melted mountains. The twinkling of the stars came above her. Would either of the two moons rise this night or would it be spent in blackness? She did not consciously sleep but let the feelings of urgency and fear slip from her into the night. She could do little until the morning.

◊◊◊

Dawn rose harshly into the sky – the sun was overly intense and dazzling. Parlòp looked around her. They were all in the same positions as they'd been the evening before. Taraganam was beside Kalanomena's body. She had stopped crying now but sat there, cross-legged, beside him. Blood had flowed from his wound and her blue robes were covered in a dark red stain. She did not seem to notice.

Caresma was lying just a few feet from her, just pushing himself upright on his elbows. He was gazing at the wize woman as if he still wondered what to do. Krasne was sitting near Parlòp, the firestick cradled in his hands.

Parlòp rose, feeling that she should do something. She stepped back into the gentle claws of the beast. Then she stopped, not wanting to abandon Saimar's corpse. She looked down at herself. She was dressed now in rags, for she had ripped and torn her shift into many pieces to staunch his wounds. It did not matter. She pulled the remains into some semblance of propriety. She did not care what any runneler saw or thought. But Kelsar men were unseemly in such matters.

She looked out at the dawn-lit landscape. Were they lost here now – forever? 'Is this the Stone Desert?'

'Caresma said it was,' said Krasne from beside her. 'I saw the edge of it once, far in the south of the Karsar lands. We were sent there to fight when I was young and the greatest of the towers of the wize was Naragorema. But he got above himself. There was an alliance against him between the then Kelsari and the other Karsar towers.' He sighed as if remembering something bitter and hard. 'We fought with the sorcery of phantasy and with sword and we brought him down. His forest lands bordered the desert and I saw it from afar.' He gestured around them. '"And mountains melted like tallow . . ."' He looked around them, indicating peremptorily with his hand.

'Will we not die?'

'Who knows. No one crosses the Har Kolem and lives. The Aallesar of the lakelands have a story that Vaallesar, the founder of their kingdom, did. But it is not known whether such a person ever existed. It was hundreds of years ago in the dark days following the ravaging. Little is remembered from that time – only myths.' He snorted. 'But at least we are out of those accursed vaults – free to breathe air again. Even poisoned air.'

Parlòp looked across at this Kelsara. This was a man who needed to do the right thing and unfailingly tried to find it. 'What do we do, Krasne Kelsara? These wize will agree on nothing if left to themselves.'

He looked without any hope but then he straightened and the military man of before returned. He hefted the firestick. 'Let's try,' he said.

Parlòp walked forward with a determination she did not feel but something had to be said, be done. The shadow skittered away from her as she disturbed it. She reached Taraganam. Caresma sat beside her, uncomfortable and uncomforting, but still in the role of protector.

From what? Us?

No one spoke. Krasne stood beside Parlòp. She glanced at him; his face was set, the military man ready for whatever came. He was the only one who looked at all in charge of the moment – more than Parlòp felt anyway. This was a mission adrift, a useless quest. Yet here they were.

They all waited – for, she realised, Parlòp to speak.

'Where are we? And why are we here?' she said.

Caresma spoke. 'It is real,' he said, not answering her question.

Parlòp felt that somewhere in all this she, and they all, had lost the sense of what was real, what was true. Did it even matter anymore? All that mattered was life.

Krasne spoke, brusque and in command once more. 'Taraganam Karsara! What are we doing here? Why have you brought us to this place of death?'

The Karsara woman turned lazily as if she had not remembered there was anybody there but her dead love and herself. 'I know it, this place – I knew it. I was born in a river village that bordered the last forests before the desert. We could see this poisoned wilderness glowing above them at night. One time, when I was young and foolish, I went with friends and gazed on it, at this. So I willed us here.' She shook her head.

'How can we know for sure it is real? Have you catapulted us to some substitute world?'

'This is the real desert,' said Caresma firmly. 'She dreamed into existence a dimensional quantum phase... I mean, like a tunnel... to transport us here. The crystal is an energeia source. You can create matter from it, making your dreams solid, or use it as a power source for other things you can imagine doing. Kalanomena was not creating reality. He was exploiting it.'

What words were these? How did he know these things?

'Why are we here though, Taraganam?' said Krasne. 'Why the desert of death?'

'It was the only place that came to me. I wanted to get him away from Turganamena. To make him safe... to make us safe. But it was pointless. He was gone.' She looked back at Kalanomena's body and then slowly, tenderly, bent forward to hold him.

'Is this your idea of safety?' said Parlòp hotly.

Caresma gave her a strong look. 'Have peace, mystic. She needed time.' He looked very powerful for a moment, almost as if he glowed. 'She needed space. And we needed to get away from the tower. Turganamena must not get his hands on the crystal. We cannot allow this technology to . . .' He paused, looking for an instant as if he doubted his own words – or regretted them. 'This is a sorcery that should not be in the world. The power to create reality, armies, whatever you wish is not to be permitted. We must destroy the crystal.'

'How can we do that?' said Krasne who, from his tone, agreed heartily with the idea.

'If we destroy it, how will we get back?' Parlòp said. 'Would you have us walk out of this place?'

Caresma glared at her.

Taraganam was still bent over the body of Kalanomena, but the crystal was firmly in her fist. They all looked down at her. Regardless of whatever she, Krasne or Caresma thought, Taraganam held the crystal and she was the one to decide.

'We must burn him. His body . . . he deserves a proper cremation.' She looked up with red-rimmed eyes, then looked down at him again. 'But we've done this already . . . He is twice dead. I must twice mourn him. But we cannot . . . leave him.' She looked at the crystal in her fist. 'Can I summon fire with this?'

Caresma sighed. 'I think he was already dead, Taraganam. I think this one was the copy who killed his creator. This was the one full of ambition and hatred, the one who was the shadow, the darkness in his ka. There was little left but desire and ambition. He killed the Kalanomena that you cared for . . . he killed his truth. There is only one of any of us. He was lost in evil.'

Taraganam looked up at the wize. 'But we must annihilate . . . his body must be burnt. It is the tradition of both our peoples. Whichever was the real Kala . . . we must burn this Kala as we did the other. Whichever was true, whichever was false. They were both him.' She stopped and wept again.

Krasne stepped forward and leant down. 'I can burn his body,

Taraganam. I can use this firestick as I did with Barces.' He paused. 'And wish I could have with Tarsh . . .'

'You will drain its power if you keep using it,' said Caresma. 'It is not going to last forever.'

'But he must be cremated,' Taraganam screamed it at him. 'The way of those who are wize. It is the kaioo.' She looked up at the Kelsar guard and rose shakily to her feet. 'Do it, Kelsara. Take him from me . . .'

Krasne looked at her with sympathy but he levelled the firestick, pointing it at the body.

Caresma looked fierce. 'You . . .' he began.

The Kelsara fired and the body of Kalanomena was enveloped in fire. He burst into blue flame and quickly turned to ash. The embers drifted off and the firestick sputtered, the flame from it guttering and dying. In the quiet breeze, the mad wize floated away in spirals of whiteness.

Krasne took his finger from the trigger.

Caresma, glaring at him, shook his head slowly. 'I did say it would not last forever. Well, perhaps it is best that the technology, that sorcery is not in the hands of such a flawed people.'

Krasne looked irritated. He turned and pointed the firestick away from them all. He pulled the trigger but, as Parlòp expected, nothing happened. He shrugged and threw the weapon to the ground.

'We would be dead without it. It served us well. The warriors of Turganamena would have killed Parlòp and me many times without it.'

Parlòp turned and looked back at the body of the allarg. She was sad, in a strange way, that there was no longer any fire to burn away the body of her friend. But it was not the tradition of her people to burn the dead. Cremation was the barbaric tradition of the river and tower. The Solpsar returned their dead to the swamp that gave them birth, to the marshland that fed and housed them.

They believed that, by that, they gave their lives back to the ground, which would then give birth to more life and many.

She walked away from them. Back with the allarg, she knelt and stretched her hands out across his back. Saimar must stay here instead. If there was any life left in this toxic place it could take him to itself. If not, he would, by his decay, leave some of the existence that had been his to be a source of new life in the place of death. That was their way. She looked up.

Krasne was gazing down at her. 'Sorry,' he said, seemingly discerning the thoughts that had been in her head.

'It matters not,' she said. 'It is not our way. We allow decay. We return ourselves to the world.'

Krasne looked unhappy. 'I know . . . but . . .'

'We must destroy the crystal,' said Caresma again. 'We cannot permit this in the world.'

Taraganam, still holding the gem, pulled it closer to her chest. 'No. Kalanomena gave his life to this dream. The ancient myth that truth can be created, that we make our own reality – we can make the world in our own likeness. We can do good with this thing. We have only seen the evil. Kala was led astray by his ambition and his ka was fractured. Perhaps it was broken before he ever laid his hand on this power. His obsession broke him long ago. My ka is not broken. I could feed the hungry. We could all be rich. There would be no poverty. We could stop all war. No one would dare stand against anyone who could conjure armies – from nothing.'

'And you could destroy the world too,' said Krasne. 'Power has strange effects on people. They cease to be . . . kind.'

Taraganam looked away from him, turning to stare northwards. 'I must think. I need to . . . his dream must not die. We can do good. I can do great things for the world.' Her face took on an inspired look. 'So, we must go somewhere. I cannot return to the tower of Turganamena. I cannot return home.' She paused, and

Parlòp could see her face working.

'There are no lands where you will be safe once people understand what you have. Lake, plain or mountain people. Give me the crystal and I shall destroy it.' Caresma took a step forward.

Parlòp thought he was about to take it by force. Taraganam thought the same thing because she recoiled, raising her fist.

Like ripples in water the world wavered.

Parlòp looked up in resignation. As she did, she thought she saw a man standing on one of the western hills of the desert. He looked as if he had been watching them. But the world flowed away; the melted mountains of the stone desert were gone and the man retreated into imagination.

It could not have been. He was not there.

The desert is just a place of death.

The world recombined. They had returned to the vaults of Vyderbo.

Had they ever truly left? She wondered.

Chapter 11

*'Before you is life and death,
abundance and destitution.
Choose Life'*

After Devarim

The strange lights of the pillars revealed again the discarded riches of Kalanomena's greed. They were back – trapped – in the vaults. She gazed at the others with unutterable hopelessness. They all stood in the order they had stood in the poisoned desert. Despondent, Parlòp settled to the floor.

Would they ever get out? Would they survive this craziness? Perhaps everything was a dream. But Saimar was dead and Kalanomena too. So it had to be real. Or were they lost in some imagined vision? Was truth simply a form of insanity? Perhaps she was still in her swamp temple, lost in utter madness.

'Why did you bring us back here?' said Krasne forcefully.

'Where else?' said Taraganam. 'We need to be secure.'

'We must destroy the crystal to be safe,' said Caresma.

'No,' said Taraganam fiercely. 'Kala's greed led him astray.' She hesitated, suddenly crestfallen. 'He always wanted more than he had – knowledge, influence and power. We could have been happy, he and I. I could never persuade him differently. He always strived for an ephemeral... greatness.' She seethed. 'I must destroy everything he made and do good.'

'This gem cannot be permitted,' said Caresma.

Would he try to take it by force? Would he do so before she could act to retaliate? Parlòp sensed a fight coming. What could she do?

As if in response to the very thought, Taraganam growled and brandished her fist. The lights of the gem twinkled and shadowed between her whitened fingers. In a flash of light, all the riches that surrounded them disappeared. Parlòp sighed. *Riches are a mist that appears for a little time and then vanishes.*

A series of confused emotions crossed Taraganam's face. 'For Kala ... the good I do will be his legacy. He died for this power. There must be a way to use this power to build up – not to tear down.'

'"A day to cast away, and a day to gather together,"' said Krasne.

He was quoting something, Parlòp knew that, but she could not remember what – some text of the river people. There is a day to gather the boats and a day to break away.

Taraganam knew the quote as well for she nodded fiercely and turned abruptly away. 'I need to think,' she said. 'I must not act in haste.'

Parlòp did not think she was stable anymore. Did the gem do that to everyone? Take them to breaking point and beyond?

'We need to destroy it,' said Caresma. 'There is no way this world can cope with such power.'

Parlòp could tell he knew he was not winning. The shadow beast had hunkered down beside her. She turned and looked at it, reaching out a hand to brush one of its many clawed paws. It recognised the gentleness of the action; she felt through the staff its deep understanding. She wished she was alone. She wished that all these others would go off to deal with whatever their concerns were, whatever their priorities were, and she could just take the shadow beast and retreat to her temple. She cared no longer if the Kelsar and the Karsar went to war. She cared not for the commands of her king, be he excellent or her Grandee. She just wanted peace.

Taraganam was moving. She walked into the complex of rooms on this level of the vaults. The floors were now empty. Caresma followed her, talking. He looked upset and, she could tell, was close to releasing his anger. She felt a fury deep within him. Something in him despised the whole world. He thought himself, knew himself, to be superior to them all.

He would try, surely, to wrestle the gem from Taraganam. But it did not matter to Parlòp which of these insane wize held the gem. It was cursed. They were cursed. If he destroyed it, that would be for the good. But none of them could bear to do it once it was in their hands.

They had walked off. Krasne sat down beside her. 'What shall we do, mystic?'

She shrugged. 'I find it hard to care. So much has been lost – your men, Saimar my allarg, and the madman himself. Will we ever get out? Are we not trapped here until Taraganam, or Caresma, decides where else they will transport us?'

Krasne pointed towards the far archway. 'Well, we haven't found what is through the far doorway. The stairs should lead further up. We might still find the way out, via the second staircase. Remember'

Parlòp looked over at the far arch. The Kelsar guard was right. She had forgotten. This had been the hope that had brought them here. She looked over at the doorway and then back at the guard. 'Maybe it will lead to another . . . to more horror.'

'I understand that – but we must try. I must try. I want to return to my woman. I want to hold my child. I will not await my fate at the whim of these wize.'

Parlòp nodded. 'I want my swamp as well. Let's go on then, Kelsara, and find what we find.' She turned and looked in the direction that Taraganam and Caresma had gone. She could not see either of them. They had walked into the complex of rooms on the left side of the hallway. She wasn't sure she even wanted them to return.

'Shall we bring the wize?' she said.

Krasne rose to his feet. 'I say go on without them. We can always come back. We know where they are. If Taraganam magics them away, then maybe that is safer.' He laughed shortly.

'We might be free of them . . . but if there is no way out ahead and Taraganam leaves then we are trapped here until we die.' Parlòp stroked the head of the shadow beast beside her. They would need food soon. And water. She could not remember the last time she had eaten.

Krasne walked forward. 'They deserted us first, left us here without a word. So, we scout – alone.'

Parlòp nodded. The Kelsara was right – as always. She rose to her feet and voiced the shadow beast to come with her. Fretfully, it skittered after her as she strode to the exit; Krasne walked beside them. They reached the arch.

She stared up the steps and glanced at Krasne. The light from the pillars streamed into the landing but Parlòp could see that it was dark further up. She wondered where she had put her torch and rummaged in her wet-leather pack.

But Krasne had already produced his and was striking a tinderbox to light it. Perhaps Krasne's torch would be enough. It would leave both her hands free to wield the staff at any threats. And Krasne still had a sword scabbarded at his waist.

When his torch was alight they climbed. The light spilt ahead of them. There was a landing, as before, where the stairs turned, and a thick layer of dust on the steps. No one had passed this way for some while.

They mounted the second set of stairs, the beast skulking behind. With its fearsome claws, it should have been leading the way. She worried if somewhere deep inside its mind was the knowledge of what awaited them. But its mind, like most beasts, was not penetrable to that level. She knew their feelings. She could not find their memories. Perhaps they did not keep them the way people did. Parlòp knew it felt unsure of what lay ahead – but then it was always timid.

A quiver of fear ran down Parlòp's back. The beast, behind her, whimpered as it felt her fear flowing to it through the staff. She couldn't stop herself slowing and hesitating.

Krasne, next to her, paused too and seemed to understand her caution. 'We must discover what is there,' he said and drew his sword, raising the torch. 'The dust on the floor tells me that Kalanomena did not come this way. Surely there will be no danger created by the accursed gem.'

She smiled faintly. 'Perhaps . . . but who knows what else?'

They walked up the steps together and rounded the final corner. She saw light. Ahead of them was a deep chasm, a large circular hole in the floor. On the far side of the abyss were men with torches. As they arrived the men shouted to each other. People appeared behind them. Parlòp could not conceive who they were.

What was going on? Had Turganamena come?

Then she realised they were river people, Kelsar. She felt a rush of relief, followed abruptly by concern. What would they do? There were hasty movements on the other side of the chasm and arrows flew towards her. Others were shouting. Parlòp retreated and instinctively raised her staff to fend the arrows off. They thudded to the ground before her, skidding and breaking on the stone floor. She backed into the shadow beast and realised that they were shooting at it.

'Stop!' shouted Krasne, retreating. 'It is Krasne.' He looked around wildly as more arrows flew past him. They were getting their range. The arrows would hit home soon. A look of understanding passed over his face. 'Stop! The beast will not attack! The Solpsara mystic has tamed it.'

Parlòp had backed into the stairwell, pulling the beast with her. It was whining and mewling – its fear flowed to her like a physical blow. She retreated down the first few stairs. She was no longer able to see the Kelsar. Two more arrows thudded through the archway to the ground behind Krasne. Then they ceased.

Parlòp took a few steps up, holding the staff between her and the beast to stop him from advancing. She risked a glance.

Krasne had walked forward to the edge of the chasm, exposing himself to attack. 'I am Officer Krasne. Do not shoot.'

'The monster – what was that?' called a man.

Krasne waved his sword impatiently. 'It is born of shadow, the creation of an insane Karsara. The swamper mystic has tamed it. The Kelsari himself sent her with me. Leave it be. Where are your officers?'

'It is not real, sir? A phantasm?' shouted the man.

'Real enough,' replied Krasne, 'but let it alone.'

Parlòp heard more indistinct shouting. She ordered the beast to remain out of view and stepped through the archway to stand behind Krasne. He glanced at her and smiled. 'They will obey. But keep the beast out of sight.'

Parlòp nodded. She had already done that.

She looked down at the pit before them. The chasm was circular. It was not as deep as she had first thought, but still at least thirty feet down. The sides were smooth and not stone or earth – something else. It was not simply gouged out of the ground. It had been built; it had once contained something. There were ledges on its walls, metallic brackets, rusty with age, down the sides. Parlòp decided that at one time the pit had housed three concentric circular devices that rested on the ledges, secured in the brackets. Whatever they had been, each circle was smaller than the one above it, so the hole narrowed towards the bottom. She wondered what it had been. Some magical device of the ancients – no doubt taken when so many of the forgotten mysteries of this vault had been removed. It was unfortunate that they had missed the most powerful device of all – the crystal.

She glanced behind them and wondered if Caresma had persuaded Taraganam to attempt to destroy the jewel. The power was too great. Parlòp agreed it could not be permitted in the world.

But Taraganam would not listen to her, a swamper. No wize would. They were arrogant like that – river or tower, it made no difference.

She looked back to the pit. It would be easy to get into it by jumping perhaps from ledge to ledge until you reached the bottom. But it would not be as easy to climb back out on the other side, even with some of the brackets to grasp and use as handholds. However, the Kelsar had lowered a ladder from their side to the nearest and highest of the ledges. It was a flimsy thing but, with many of them, they might construct a way out. Or perhaps with ropes?

She glanced to the sides of the chasm, wondering if they could make their way around it. Narrow circular ledges surrounded the pit, blocked by cramped doors, two on each side. They were metal – heavy, thick – but only slightly rusted by passing time. Between the two doors on both sides, she saw more rooms.

She wondered if she should run over and try the doors. But surely that would have been the first thought of the Kelsar, to make a precarious way around the hole rather than into it. Therefore, surely, they were locked or sealed – inoperable after the passage of time.

She was wondering about trying anyway when there was a disturbance on the far side and new people, all men, appeared.

One of them was military in bearing and Krasne looked immediately deferential. The other was the Dawen – Torgane was his name – the short, hassled-looking man she had first met inside the Kelsari's palace. The one with the excessive daggers – all for show, no doubt.

'Is that you, guard Krasne?' said the Dawen. 'We came in search of your party.'

'What has happened? Report, officer!' said the other man.

Parlòp guessed who this man was – Confluent Traizer. He was

their warlord, the head of all the armed forces of the Kelsar, and Krasne's ultimate superior. Parlòp had never seen him. But he had led many attacks on her people. It was not good that he had come.

Krasne replied to him. 'What hasn't happened, my lord? We have been through many trials. Riverguards Barces and Tarsh are dead. The mystic Parlòp, myself and the two wize survive. We have discovered that by a vile magic, Kalanomena duplicated himself. Then the copy killed the original. He has brought into the world a new terrible power – the ability to create dreams, to make real the phantasies of the wize.'

Parlòp saw a stir as he spoke the words. She wondered if it had been wise, so easily and quickly, to reveal the powers they had unearthed. It was a terrible ability. If it became well known it would attract all sorts of people with bad motives.

But perhaps Krasne had no choice.

'We came to find you,' said Dawen Torgane. 'The other way was blocked by a cave-in. This way is blocked by this chasm, but we have sent for more ladders and ropes so that we can bridge this pit.'

'We know of the blockage, my lord Dawen. We were on the other side when the roof collapsed. We reached this side by a perilous journey.'

Krasne glanced at Parlòp and spoke, not loud enough for his Kelsar superiors to hear. 'We must tell the others that our rescue is here.' A troubled look crossed his features. 'Tell Caresma and Taraganam that there will be a great . . . interest in the gem and its powers. Caresma is right. It must be destroyed. Go, tell them so. I will aid the rescue here as best I can.' He leaned towards her, speaking even more quietly. 'Tell them to hurry and destroy it. It must not get out of the vaults.'

Parlòp nodded, but carefully, so it was not obvious to those presumably watching them that he had suggested anything. She turned abruptly on her heel and passed through the archway.

Ordering the beast to follow her, she descended several steps before she realised that she needed her torch alight.

'The mystic will fetch the others. They are just below,' Krasne called above her.

Parlòp pulled her torch from her wet-leather pack, but she could not light it. She had not carried any tinder and flint for, despite the wet-leather pack, they so often got damp. She would need another torch to light it from.

But it did not seem a good idea to return and use Krasne's. She was not sure quite why; it was just inviting a command from the far side for her to stay. With the darkened torch in one hand, the staff in the other, and the shadow beast following her, she ran as swiftly down the stairs as she could in the semi-darkness. The faint light of Krasne's torch faded but once she reached the landing below and turned, she saw lights from the chamber below. It was not an easy trip, but she managed and reached the bottom without falling. The shadow beast was unaffected. She wondered if it could see the dark. She knew so little of its capabilities.

She stepped into the hallway below, so recently piled with riches beyond counting. And that framed the whole problem. If the wealth had remained, it would have overbalanced the economy of the river people and indeed the other peoples of the world. If the Kelsar had become fabulously wealthy they would have every mercenary in the world racing to fight for them. They would dominate everyone all too easily. And the swamp people would be first into thraldom. She did not like the idea of a world dominated by the river people. It would be equally as bad if any one of the peoples was able to lord it over the others. Be they tower, mountain, river or swamp. Her world survived in precarious balance; no nation dominated the others.

Parlòp wanted only to return to her swamp and be left in peace. But to achieve that, she could not countenance the gem in anyone's hands. The crystal could not be allowed.

She could not see Caresma and Taraganam anywhere. Where could they be? She found no sign of them in the hall or either of the large rooms to the side. They were perhaps further in. A complex set of chambers stretched beyond the first room.

She walked forward, crossing the room. They had gone that way. The beast skittered along beside her, happy, she felt, to be back in a place it understood. It was surreal to think that this cursed place was the closest it had to home.

She had reached the far side where a broken doorway led to a corridor. Down the corridor were doors, some intact, some broken. At the far end of the corridor was a half-open doorway. Through it, she saw a very bright light.

Taraganam was screaming in her native tongue – words of defiance and fear. Parlòp ran forward. Caresma was trying to seize the gem.

Chapter 12

*'Hear the command of life;
give ear, and learn.'*

After Sirath

Parlòp dashed through the doorway and saw ahead the huge curve of an amphitheatre. Taraganam was kneeling at the bottom. A giant Caresma was towering over her, shouting. How did he get so big? Surrounding his form was a strange glow. Has some strange fire set him alight?

Taraganam screamed. 'I will not! What are you? You are no man.'

Caresma's form at once grew twice or more times larger. He dominated the scene. He rained an ethereal blue fire down upon Taraganam. She created a strange umbrella of darkness over herself and the bluish flames emanating from Caresma were sucked into the blackness.

Parlòp ran forward – she could not stop herself. She shouted incoherent words of fear and challenge. She brandished the staff before her as if it could prevent the attack and ran down the steps towards the two wize. Was he a wize? She did not know why she went. She could not fully comprehend what she was seeing or doing. What would she do when she got there?

The gigantic glowing Caresma swung round and glared its fiery gaze at her. 'Why did you return? I could have destroyed her. Now I must kill you both.'

The words spoken, Caresma melted away into a massive column of light and heat. Flames cascaded down onto Taraganam. The umbrella shield expanded to a great hemisphere of darkness, surrounding and protecting her from the attack. Parlòp reached the bottom of the steps and stopped. She stood there, staff held sideways as if she could do something useful with it. She was unsure what.

Words sounded. She could not tell who spoke. 'Give it to me! It is not permitted. You are not ready. We must save you from yourselves.'

Taraganam screamed some other words in the Karsar tongue. The hemisphere of darkness swept out from her and up. The monstrous column of heat retreated from it hastily. *Darkness is a threat?*

'Fool!' the bodiless voice screamed. 'I shall return. You will not stand against us. You will not wield this technology. Give it to me now. You can be saved.'

The fiery pillar dissolved into a ball of light and heat and sped up the broken rows of the theatre, passing very close to Parlòp. She felt the heat from it scorching her flesh and raised her wooden staff instinctively. Strangely, the heat lessened. The ball of glowing light and heat streaked up the amphitheatre and out of the doorway. Taraganam screamed.

Parlòp turned. The Karsara wize had fallen to her knees. Parlòp cursed some choice words in the Solpsar language. 'What was that?'

The shield of darkness had moved outwards, curving up and folding into itself like a shadow dissolving in the midday sun. Parlòp stepped forward. A weakened and shocked wize woman was left, kneeling, still clutching the gem, her fist surrounded by a swirling light and darkness, flickering over her whitened fingers.

Parlòp swore again in Solpsar. 'What just happened?'

Taraganam looked up. She looked bemused, surprised by Parlòp's presence. She stared at her blankly for several moments before she seemed to comprehend what she was seeing. The look of confusion slipped slowly from her features. 'He tried to take it from me! It tried to take it from me.' She paused and slumped awkwardly forward. 'What was he? He was no man. No wize has such powers.' She spoke the words and crumpled to the ground.

Parlòp did not reply. Nor did she move. What was to be said? She turned and gazed back up the serried rows of the theatre. They were strewn with the remains of rotted broken wood and rusting metal. There would have been seats here once, she thought, the notion coming unbidden. She took a few steps up as if to follow the strange monster that Caresma had become, revealed himself to be. What was to be done? She stopped and stared up at the doorway through which the monster had departed.

'Will it ... he come back?' Oddly she felt even thinking the thought would bring the monstrous glowing Caresma back. She turned back to Taraganam still hunched, kneeling on the floor.

'What was he?' Taraganam said ponderously.

Parlòp felt the shock draining from her. Thought was slow in returning. 'They say ... the myths say the makkuz were creatures of light and heat. That they could, at will, appear as ordinary men and women. Could he be one?'

Taraganam gazed at her, a vague look of confusion crossing her face. For a moment she looked as if she was considering how to rise to her feet but did not know how to do it. She shook her head. 'But Caresma has been the Fount of the Wize order of the Kelsar for many years. I have met him several times.' She looked up at Parlòp. 'How could he be one of the monsters from the skies? The Hraddas ... the makkuz came over eight hundred years ago.'

'How else could he do that, Taraganam? There have been a few times when he seemed to know things ... to do things that no wize could. I never had time to discover ... to sort out what was going on. We lurched from one crisis to another.' She took a few steps towards Taraganam, wondering if she should offer to help her up. The wize woman still clutched the perilous gem. Would she strike her down?

'Will he come back? It ...' Taraganam struggled back to an

upright, kneeling position.

Parlòp shook her head. 'He left because he could not best you.' She paused as a terrible thought occurred to her. 'But ... what if there more of them? Did he say he was going to fetch ... reinforcements? Are there makkuz in the world still – watching, ready to destroy us? He said *we* – he said ... he would return.'

Taraganam paled. 'I could not ... Can I beat more of them?'

Parlòp slowly shook her head. 'This is why we must destroy the gem. It is a threat – it attracts too much danger. Everything evil in the world will come to take it from you – makkuz, tyrants, all the ravenous volfs of people.'

Parlòp noticed the shadow beast was not with her.

A wave of panic filled her. *Has it been killed?* She turned about, seeking. Then, calming, she realised she still felt its presence. She ran up a few of the steps and then she saw it. It was right at the top of the ranks of broken seating, hiding in the furthest corner of the theatre. It was bent low as if it did not want to be seen. She ordered it to come to her. The beast rose and came but slowly, reluctantly, looking around in fear. It came and stood before her. She reached out with a gentle hand and stroked its head, running her fingers across its vicious teeth. She smiled as the beast reacted to her, pushing gently against her hand.

She turned. Taraganam had risen to her feet. She was recovering her composure. Her clenched fist holding the jewel was loose at her side.

'I did not expect ... Caresma was simply arguing with me, to destroy it – to lose it from the world when we could do so much with its power. Good things – not evil or insane. My Kala lost his mind to it. We must somehow redeem his memory by using his dreams to ... make the world a better place.' She walked forward a step. 'Then he attacked.'

Parlòp sighed. Taraganam was wrong. This thing was uncontrollable. It was beyond anyone's skill to defend it. But this was not the moment to argue further with the Karsara. If she persisted, the wize could kill her.

Parlòp relaxed and said. 'The Kelsar are above us. They have come down the other staircase and found the way to us. There is a large pit between them and us that we must bridge before they can reach us.' She hesitated. Should she speak? Was there any point? 'Taraganam, the Kelsar as well may try to take this power to themselves.' She could not prevent herself from saying, 'Taraganam, maybe we should not let this thing be in the world. It is too much power.'

Taraganam backed away. 'You would destroy it too.'

Parlòp shook her head. 'I have no interest in it. But your dreams of doing good will sour. The real world is not like that. It will be a better place without this power. Magic to make our dreams reality. To create all our nightmares of violence. It will overbalance our world and,' she hesitated, 'if the makkuz think they must destroy it, they too will come back to take it from you. He said as much.'

Taraganam glared at her. 'I will be ready next time. I can fight any enemy with the powers this gem gives.' And there it was – the arrogance of the wize had returned to this Karsara.

Parlòp shrugged. 'If you will not destroy it, then be ready. The Caresma-makkuz will return with more of the hidden watchers. The Kelsar will bridge the chasm above us soon enough. Once the Kelsari or his warlord the Confluent understand the power of this thing, they too will want it. You will face multiple rivals. The war that results will threaten my people as well. The warlord of the Kelsar has fought many times against us. And it threatens your people too. The Karsar will not stand by and watch the Kelsar grow strong. Turganamena rules the Karsar as the strongest of the towers. Will he welcome you back after—' Parlòp stopped talking. Taraganam was not listening.

She turned slowly round and stroked the claws of the shadow

beast beside her. 'Very well. Let's go and meet the Kelsar. You must find the way down this river of consequence for yourself, Taraganam Karsara. I hope you find the true stream.'

Taraganam thrust the gem into some hidden pocket in her robe and looked back at Parlòp. 'Yes, let us go. And not tell them of the power of—'

'Krasne has already told them,' Parlòp said, interrupting. 'The Confluent Traizer is there. Krasne reported to him that Kalanomena found a device with the power to make phantasy real. He is a man under authority – perhaps he had no choice.' She sighed. 'They know, Karsara wize. They know.'

Taraganam shook her head. 'We can do good, Solpsara. Do you not see that? We can fill the whole world with everything it needs and wants. No one needs to be hungry ever again. My family was poor and needy until my potential to be one of the wize was discovered. Through my new powers and the support of my Lord Turganamena, they were fed and given refuge. I can do even more with this. I can free the world of poverty. No one will want to oppose me when they see the benefits of its power. We can make the world as it should have been. We can break every weapon of war, destroy everyone who tries to dominate. That is why the makkuz sought to destroy it. We can make everything the way it was, the way it could have been. We can reverse the destruction they wrought in the ravaging. How can we destroy such a thing of hope – a device to make all our dreams true?'

'Dreams, yes,' said Parlòp, 'and nightmares too. You underestimate the greed of people. I do not want to live in such a world as you would make. Leave me be. I will return to my swamp.' She turned on her heel and strode up the stairs to the door leading out of the amphitheatre. Soon she would be free. Soon she would leave the river and immerse herself in the mud of the swamp. Then she would be clean . . . clear of the machinations of the ambitious.

Taraganam followed. She heard her step behind.

The wize spoke again. 'You will understand when you see the marvels I will make.'

Parlòp ignored her. Through the staff, Parlòp sensed the confidence that filled the wize woman. Doubts, if she had any, were pushed deep down inside. She wanted nothing but for Kalanomena's overweening desire to be seen as a good thing.

This was not going to end well.

They needed to swim on and see where the stream went. Parlòp knew she had no choice. Perhaps her cynicism was misplaced. Maybe common sense would prevail. Maybe Taraganam would come, in her own time, to an understanding of the true nature of the world – and its danger. Maybe she would stop caring either way.

Parlòp reached the end of the corridor and stepped through into the large room. As she approached the central hall, Krasne appeared with his sword drawn looking fierce and worried.

As he saw them, he cursed. 'What was that?'

'What—?'

'A fireball came up the stairs from here and rushed past me, over the chasm and through the Kelsar guards and . . . out of the vaults.'

'It was Caresma . . .' said Taraganam from behind.

'We believe he was a makkuz . . . or something like it,' added Parlòp. 'Perhaps he was never a man. He revealed himself—'

Taraganam interrupted. 'He tried to take the gem from me. He said it must be destroyed.' She walked forward to stand beside Parlòp.

'Yes, it must be destroyed,' said Krasne fiercely, although as he said it he sheathed his sword. 'It is too much power for us – for you, for anyone.'

'You as well?' said Taraganam. 'Do you not see the good we can do?'

'Only the harm. Do you not see that its possession will lead to war?'

'I can stop any opposition with a quick conjuring of a new reality. Perhaps there are no limits to what I can change.'

'Like Kalanomena...' said Krasne. Taraganam's face collapsed and tears rolled again down her strong features.

Taraganam was doomed. Parlòp did not feel much sympathy for her, despite her loss of a man dear to her. She was being foolish, but whilst the gem was in her control there was little to be done. Taraganam wanted, needed perhaps, to redeem Kalanomena's madness. It was mere foolishness.

'What is the situation above – with the pit?' said Parlòp, preferring to talk of more hopeful things – the possibility of escape, of running away and returning to the safety of the swamp, to her animals, to her temple.

Krasne looked at her. 'The ladders and ropes have arrived. They have constructed a way down on their side and are working to get ladders up to our side. They will be with us soon enough. I was sent by my lord Confluent Traizer to seek the source of the fireball.'

'Did it... he hurt anyone?' said Parlòp, thinking as she did that she should probably have asked sooner.

'No... it seemed to be made of light rather than heat. It just swept past us. Do the makkuz exist then? I thought them a myth.'

Parlòp shrugged. 'They were... they are. But the myths say that they watch us still, ready to punish any presumption. So it will be until the magician kings return. The legend has it that they were beings of light and heat. If he is not one, he must be something like it. Who knows—'

Krasne interrupted. 'If he was a makkuz, can it bring more of the foul Hraddas, the monsters of the skies to assail us?'

'Probably... I do not know.' She shrugged impatiently and made to walk past. 'I don't know what is happening anymore.

Where will this lead? The world will have to look after itself. This mystic wants to go home and never leave my temple again.' She moved past the Kelsara guard and went to the stairs.

The shadow beast followed her closely and she heard Krasne and Taraganam following her. They did not speak; Krasne did not attempt to argue with Taraganam. Was he too resigned to what was going to happen? Even if she tried to seize the gem, Taraganam would be able to kill her before her paltry powers could overwhelm her. Even the shadow beast wouldn't strike her down before she could retaliate. Anyway, Parlòp could not risk the beast. It deserved to live and not be wasted in some futility – like a broken weapon hurled in a deep pool. The world would have to look after itself. Parlòp did not care. Her swamp beckoned. She would go home.

She reached the top of the stairs. The far side of the pit was now festooned with ropes and ladders and several guards were making their way down. She ordered the beast to remain on the landing, in the shadows, and walked forward.

She reached the edge and looked down. The Kelsar had placed many ladders up her side also. They needed only one more, which they were just putting in place, to have bridged the gap. The guards climbing up out of the pit looked up at her. Their faces were questioning as if they wondered what the swamper mystic would do, or was it some puzzlement as to why she was there? Perhaps they were not aware the Kelsari had summoned her. Runnelers were all prejudiced against her kind.

Krasne appeared beside her and bending down took hold of the final ladder and steadied it. The leading riverguard climbed the last few rungs and heaved himself out, with Krasne's help, to stand beside them.

Krasne shook his hand warmly. 'You have rescued us.'

Parlòp smiled faintly. She was not sure they were rescued just yet – they were just released. They brought the danger with them.

It would spread. She turned and looked at Taraganam. It was hopeless.

Chapter 13

*'Those who choose life will have abundance,
but those who chase phantasies have no sense.'*

The Mystic Plob

Parlòp emerged into the daylight, the shadow at her side.

A huge feeling of relief flooded her. She was free. She gazed gratefully out at the ruins of Vyderbo. Until the moment she stepped out into the open air she had not realised how restricted and contained she had felt. Before this calamitous mission to Kel'Katoh, her whole life had been spent outdoors. Somehow, even the trips to the frozen land, the Tower of Turganamena and the Stone Desert had still been... strangely fixed within the constraints of the vaults. Always, in the end, they had snapped back to that reality.

They had seemed real, but they had felt false at the same time. She no longer understood. She no longer knew which of their experiences had been actual and which fantasy. Were they all real, or all fantasy? She didn't know if there was a difference. It was strange to be adrift in such a sea of unknowing. She was a mystic. It was her task to know. She did not like the feeling.

She stared out over the broken buildings that surrounded her.

It seemed real. From here, it was but a journey away from the floating city, away from the cursed river people and back to her swamp. She could run away. She could return to her temple. Surely there she would be free. There she would know where she was. She would have got out. She would be liberated.

But, will I?

She forced her attention away from the far distant swamp and looked around the ruins. Many riverguards were standing around them. The Kelsari had mobilised a great many to their rescue. She wondered why they needed this many. Were they worried about something? Was there some other threat here that she did not see? They could not have known of the gem. The Kelsar soldiers didn't approach her but left her standing alone, a few feet from the entrance to the vault. It felt like she was being avoided. She was not sure why. It would be a dislike of swamper mystics or . . . of course. It was the strange, many clawed and fanged shadow beast standing next to her.

She laughed to herself. She was the only one who knew that the beast was more scared of them than they were of it. It was constructed of fear. It had no desire to attack them. It would attack only if they threatened or cornered it. She gazed over at the Kelsar guard and felt that if it made the river people keep their distance then it was for the best.

'Swamp and river will never flow as one.'

Taraganam, Krasne and Lord Confluent emerged from the vaults, walking together. Krasne was still speaking respectfully to the warlord and Taraganam was walking beside them, looking uninterested in their conversation. She looked over at Parlòp but she did not acknowledge her or move closer.

Parlòp wondered what was in her mind. What did the Karsar wizard intend to do? What, indeed, did the Kelsari plan? But as the thoughts went through her head, Parlòp no longer cared. The world would cope without her.

She would leave, run back to her temple with the shadow. A horrible thought occurred to her. Could she leave? Could she just walk off and depart the riverlands? Or must she ask for their leave? Must she bow and scrape to these people to be permitted? She breathed out. She knew they would stop her. They would want the Kelsari to formally release her before they were happy to let her swim away.

The Dawen, Torgane, was walking out of the vaults with the rest of the riverguard at his heels. As he placed his foot on the final step a guard, looking flustered and exhausted, ran up to the warlord, Traizer.

They were but a few feet from Parlòp.

'Lord Confluent, the Kelsari sends word.' He looked up.

'What is the message?' said Traizer, brusque.

The fussy short Dawen pushed Krasne aside to stand beside the warlord as the message was given. The officer gave way quickly, stepping to the back to allow him through.

'The warning beacons have been lit, lord.' The breathless riverguard had gasped out his message. 'The Karsar have mobilised. Their armies have already breached our borders in the southern lands. Our spies report by signal that they march north, towards us. The vanguard of the Karsar will be here tomorrow, lord.' He paused again. 'There are also reports of towers from further south marching to join with them. We are invaded, Lord Confluent.'

Parlòp looked over to Krasne, a step behind his two superiors. Krasne's face was drawn, his eyes disturbed, full of doubt and uncertainty. His obedience was to these men – but his worry was with his family. It was still gnawing at him. She felt for him. He wanted to go home, just as she did, to see his woman and his child. Parlòp was not the only one who wished this was over. He also wished to simply and quickly disappear back to safety and obscurity – to normality.

The thought shamed her. She knew that Krasne would nevertheless struggle on in the contradiction between his love for his family and his obedience to his lords. And the dilemma of the crystal.

Parlòp wanted to run away and ignore it. He could not. She let a slow, anxious breath out between her teeth. Must she see this through?

The Confluent turned to Krasne. 'What do you know? Why would they attack us? How can they be moving because of the death of Kalanomena? We have not reported who killed him. It was not us.' He glanced at Parlòp and then at Taraganam, wondering if they would answer the question. At that moment the warlord did not look like the strong, confident military man he had seemed. For those moments, he looked like a worried man.

Krasne saluted and tiredly reported how they had been transported to Turganamena's tower and what Kalanomena had done there before his second death at the hands of the Wize leader.

Parlòp sighed. *And so it begins.*

Was she trapped? Would she never escape?

◊◊◊

Parlòp walked out onto the balcony. The chambers in which they had placed her were on the second storey of the palace. They were very comfortable with plush fittings and beautiful furniture, but they were still, she knew, a prison. She looked thoughtfully down at the drop and wondered if she would survive it unhurt if she leapt down.

Unfortunately, directly beneath her was the wooden deck of the pontoon on which the palace was built. It would likely hurt, landing there. And probably at the very least stun her. Even if she managed it without breaking any bones, the palace guards would be alerted by the noise of the beast and her landing. Then they would seize her. If the balcony had looked down on the river she might have done it. She could easily slip into the dark, murky depths of the main river and swim quickly away. She would be away before they could pursue her.

It did not seem to be a wise move. She turned and gazed at the shadow beast, crouched in the corner of the main room of the chambers. She wasn't sure she could order it to jump. Or if she did, whether it would. It was very unsure of its new surroundings, of these strange places to which she had taken it. There were always limits to what the most cooperative of animals would do in response to a command. The staff improved and increased the strength of her magic but even so, the beast would not wish it. It felt safe where it was, crouched in the quiet corner – away from all the strange people, alone with its Solpsar friend. Little did it know the reality.

The news of the mobilisation of the Karsar armies against the city had been met with a quick response. The riverguard had been formed up. She, the shadow, Taraganam and the Dawen had been placed in their centre.

It was merely for their protection Torgane, the Dawen, had said suavely. He had not waited for a response but turned away to chatter urgently to Taraganam. Parlòp had not paid attention to their talk. This was to constrain them, to keep her and the Karsar wize woman under control. They had arrived back at the palace promptly. The warlord, Taraganam and Krasne had hurried off to meet with the Kelsari. Parlòp had not been invited.

The Dawen, before his departure, turned to her quite hastily and fussily. 'We hope you will stay with us for the while, mystic Parlòp. If there is war coming we would send you with a message for the Solpsari. In this conflict, we would hope that peoples of swamp and river might stand together against a common foe.' He had smiled an insincere runneler smile. 'We will provide you with some rooms for your comfort while you wait.' He sharply gave orders to three Kelsar guards. 'These men will conduct you. Please await the pleasure of the Kelsari there. We will summon you as soon as we have need.' They had promptly moved to stand around her, but they gave a wide berth to the shadow.

The Dawen had quickly swung away, not inviting any response from her.

Her position was once more the lowly swamper – the dubious mystic. Her hopes were dashed. She had contemplated attacking the guards with the shadow beast and making a run for it. But this did not seem wise. The Solpsari, the excellent one, would not thank her for worsening relations with the river people by such aggressive action. After all, it had been his fear of further conflicts with the river people that had driven him to send her in the first place.

She had known she must stay. She could not help wanting to go.

So they had marched her, shadow in tow, to the rooms in which she now stood. She gazed out over the gathered pontoons, wherries and barges of the floating city.

She was not happy. She had never appreciated the politicking that surrounded all monarchs. And her king, excellent though he be, had placed her in a maelstrom not only of physical danger but political intrigue as well. By his decision, she was trapped. That galled her. She was a mystic. It was her job to understand, to puzzle out, and then to divulge. It was not to coerce or deceive people into obedience. She hoped she was an uncomplicated seeker after truth. That was her drive. Her concept of truth had taken quite a battering in the last few days. What was reality when the whim of one person could alter it?

She walked back into the room and let herself slip down into one of the luxurious chairs, the comfortable trappings of a soft prison. She put her hands on her knees and looked down at their green hue, resting on her new robe.

She had got the guards to provide her with clothing. The ripped rags that were all that remained of her shift had hardly covered her nakedness. She had seen, with annoyance, the lecherous glances of the Kelsar guards at her body as they had marched here. All knew that Kelsar men were brutes in such matters. It was annoying. Would they ever be moderate?

So she had asked for clothing when the riverguards placed her there and were setting up as sentries. A servant had come, eventually.

It was longer, a robe rather than a simple shift. Nothing you would wish to swim in. But it covered her well.

She gazed out through the balcony door at the floating city and the river beyond. She imagined rather than saw the route north to the swamp. She sighed and the shadow beast, sensing her annoyance, shifted in its place and stared at her with baleful eyes. She touched her staff and let the beast feel a peace she did not have herself.

◊◊◊

She had been there for some hours when there was a gentle knock at the door to the chamber. She rose, surprised that the Kelsari was at last summoning her. She opened the door and gazed into the eyes of a Kelsara servant. She had rarely seen anyone look so unremarkable, so nondescript. It must have been a practised look – a servant who did not want to be noticed, did not want to be censured. She looked from him to the two sentries who stood in the corridor behind. They were still there – preventing.

Parlòp looked back at the timid servant. She realised that this was not a summons from the king.

'May I have a moment of your time, mystic Parlòp?' said the servant and inclined his head in a hesitant, deeply respectful way.

'What is it?' she said. 'Does the Kelsari wish for my presence . . .' She trailed off as the servant softly, silently shook his head.

'No, Solpsara. May I come in?'

She stepped back and indicated her room. 'It is your palace, Kelsara. I am the guest.' She glanced sharply at the guards, wondering if they had picked up the stress she had put on the final word. They gazed back at her, unconcerned.

The servant entered on quiet tread, the very vision of an unimportant flunky. It was remarkable how ordinary he was. As he entered, the shadow beast stared, deeply unhappy with the newcomer. It skittered across to the balcony in panic, but stopped before actually moving outside, unsure which scared it the most, this insipid incomer or the world beyond.

The man bowed. 'Mystic Parlòp. I have come to ask your aid to prevent further unpleasantness.' He smiled a wan smile. 'May I reveal myself without causing panic?'

Parlòp inclined her head. 'Reveal yourself? Do I know you?' What could that mean?

The face of the servant dissolved and the features of Caresma appeared. 'I do not wish—'

Parlòp leapt backwards, seizing the staff from where she had laid it. She held it obliquely across her body, as if it had any chance of stopping a determined attack by a makkuz.

Caresma's face dissolved back into the form of the servant. 'I have not come to attack,' he said mildly. 'I do not, did not wish for conflict. My race does not like to reveal ourselves. We watch. I am here to avoid dispute, but this situation will make it inevitable. My true name is Poxuul. I am a . . . makkuz as you call us. I do not wish for a fight. I like and admire Kelsar people. I have lived amongst them in various guises for many centuries.'

Parlòp backed away and called the shadow to move closer to her.

The Caresma servant, Poxuul, retreated until his back was against the door from which he had entered. He was trying to make his presence less threatening. It was not working. The form of a quiet, invisible serving man still stood there but his manner now was one of authority. This truly was the formidable Caresma. Poxuul, she must call him.

Parlòp said nothing but watched him warily, her staff across her body.

'You know this device must not be allowed to stay in the control of the wize, mystic Parlòp, be they Kelsar or Karsar. I revealed myself before and have lost the work of decades creating Caresma and living his life. I have been deeply embedded amongst the Kelsar. But I had to act. She would not listen. This will not be permitted.' He paused as if struggling for the right words, or different ones. 'My lord Raczek . . . my companions on this planet will attack this place if that is what is necessary to remove this gem. This power will not be allowed.' He hesitated. 'But we do not wish to reveal our presence. I have persuaded my lord, chief amongst us, to hold off while I try to do this . . . quietly.'

'You are a makkuz! A destroyer!' Parlòp said, the angry words exploding out of her. These monsters, the Hraddas, had destroyed the ancient world. Many people had been killed – millions, it was said. And one of the killers was standing before her.

Poxuul slowly shook his head. 'We are misrepresented. You must trust me. We watch you. That is the majority of what we do. We protect your race, your world, from the malign influence of a mutual foe – an enemy to the whole universe. We prevent the worst of his excesses here. And we stop you utilising technologies of the past that you cannot hope to understand – and are not qualified to use.'

'So all this time the makkuz have been trying to help? That is not how the myths have it . . .' She drew a breath.

The formidable manner that was Poxuul and had been Caresma slipped away. The quiet, non-threatening servant returned. He gently shook his head. 'This is all secondary. Parlòp, sometimes harsh means are necessary to protect you against the wiles of our enemy. They would enslave your people for all eternity. We have to act for your good – when things go astray. You must listen to me now and not dwell on the past. For my lord Raczek, my superior, will bring our people here to destroy this whole city if that is what is necessary to save this world. We do not shy away from hard decisions. We act.'

'And now your lord will attack us.' Parlòp paused. She had heard that name, Raczek, before. It was from the mouth of a Torasara, one of the people of the plains. It had not been favourable.

'Parlòp, I seek to prevent further harm – to move discreetly. If we can extract the gem before it does any more damage that is best. I would save this world so it may join the thousands of free worlds of the galaxy. But my lord will not wait forever.' He looked across at the open entrance to the balcony. 'The risk is too great.'

Parlòp was confused. *Where is the truth here? Where is reality?* This makkuz spoke of the 'galaxy'. She remembered the legend. The myth that the stars were suns around which other worlds circled. She had always felt that it must be true, improbable as it was. But the idea was so remote from the needs of her day, the needs of the animals and trees, that she had not given it much thought – any thought if she was honest.

'Why me?' she said eventually when her heart calmed. 'As you see, I am imprisoned here for,' she laughed shortly, 'my protection.'

'They will fetch you to them, Parlòp. Trust me. I lived as a Kelsara for many years. I know them well. Chrasm, the Kelsari, is no fool. He will want every perspective on the problem laid before him. Their prejudice against a Solpsara may have locked you up, but Chrasm will not only listen to the desires of Taraganam and the reports of his guard in this thing. He will seek an . . . outside perspective.' Poxuul shook his head. 'And once he understands the power of this thing, he will desire it for himself. The Kelsari is a wize in his own right, you know. He will want this thing for his kingdom – for himself. It will give him dominion. He has always sought that.'

'It is too powerful for any to wield,' said Parlòp with feeling.

'In that, we agree. It is why I am here – because I know you understand. So help me to remove it. It must be destroyed or, at the least, removed. Raczek, my lord, will not be held back for long. He will come. He is not as patient as I.'

Parlòp gazed across at the makkuz in silence for a few moments. She could hardly credit, let alone understand this. These were the monsters who had ravaged her world. This man-thing had not denied it. He had merely excused it – as a necessity. It had been required to prevent a greater danger from some other, unknown, distant threat – a common foe to the whole universe.

Could she trust him? He was an evil monster, a Hraddas. They had been intent on preventing Parlòp's world from advancing, so the legend had it. They had killed Arnex the Warrior King. Even Franeus the High Priest and Maven honoured by the Solpsar had been vanquished. And the legend said the magician kings had all died.

She shook her head. 'Why should I trust you?'

'Trust is not necessary. We want the same thing,' said the Caresma-Poxuul thing. 'We both want it destroyed. Trust that.'

'Perhaps you just want this power for yourselves – like everyone else. Perhaps you are lying.'

The servant guffawed and, for a moment, was the powerful, strong character of Caresma again. 'I am a being of energy, of light and heat. I do not need such power. I have it already. I can form myself into any living form that I wish. I can conjure swords into existence in my hand. I can be anyone. I can take the form of men, women, animals. I do not need trinkets. We seek only to protect—' He stopped and glowered.

'What do you want me to do?' she said. It was best to let this creature think it had convinced her. She could decide what her real strategy would be later. She was not a fan of politicking, but she was not stupid. Denying this creature might result in an immediate attack by his people. She did not wish for more unnecessary deaths, even the deaths of runnelers. Krasne's words about his family flicked into her head. She did not wish them dead.

'Just watch for the opportunity to seize it. Aid me if I am forced to reveal myself. If you can, deliver it to me, then it can be destroyed.'

Parlòp considered him in silence for a moment. 'Where will you be?'

'I will be there, as near to you as I can,' he said. 'Although you may not know me. I may be neither Caresma nor this servant. I will keep this form if I can, so you know, but it may not be possible. I will be there – waiting for my . . . for our opportunity.'

The door to her room was abruptly opened. The Caresma servant backed instantly into a corner.

'The Kelsari commands your presence, swamper,' said the Kelsar officer who had stepped through the doorway unannounced. Parlòp saw three more riverguards beyond him, making five in all with her sentries. So they weren't taking any risks with a single swamper woman – and, oh yes, that vicious shadow beast they all feared.

The officer turned slowly to consider the Poxuul-servant. From his look, he had just discovered something unpleasant on his boot. 'Who are you?'

Caresma, once more the purest picture of an inconsequential lackey, said, 'I was sent to discover if the mystic required any sustenance—'

'You may go,' said the officer. 'Your presence is not required.'

Poxuul slipped quietly and silently from the room. He did not even turn and glance at Parlòp. The makkuz was confident. His point was made.

What should she do?

She looked at the surly guard officer. *I hate this.* She swore silently.

Chapter 14

*'Blazing power,
you who mould the many
so as to breathe life.'*

The Creation Song

The Kelsari was not fishing.

He was sitting on his throne. It was on a raised dais in a large audience chamber behind the room in which Parlòp had first met with the Dawen and Caresma. Parlòp decided it was meant to impress. It didn't.

He was surrounded by people. Taraganam was sitting to his right in almost as impressive a chair but placed slightly lower than the Kelsari's. The Confluent Traizer was standing on the other side looking, as always, very military and strong. There were many riverguards, officers and nobles standing around the room, none of them Parlòp knew. She didn't care that much.

She could not see Krasne. But the guard Casma who had angrily stopped her when she first arrived was there, standing at the back behind the Confluent. He looked as disgruntled as he had before.

There were servants too, moving silently through the crowd providing whatever food and drink the assembled nobles wanted. Parlòp looked around but she could not see Poxuul in the form of the nondescript servant. If he was there, as he had promised, he would be someone else. Which was he? It was quite a dizzying thought – that the makkuz infested her world, watching, ready to intervene and change things that were not acceptable to them or were dangerous to her people. She could not decide what to think about the true nature of their motives. It was weird to think that there might be more of them, people she knew, around her all the time. The thought sent a chill down her spine.

'Welcome, mystic Parlòp,' said the Kelsari. She had been taken to stand before him, like a supplicant.

She forced down the desire to say something rude. She said nothing.

'The armies of Turganamena move against us, mystic. We had hoped to avoid this result by your office of investigation.'

Parlòp stood for a moment. Was he blaming her? Was this the ploy? Everything was to be the fault of the Solpsar? It would not be the first time the Kelsar had blamed the swamp for troubles of their own making.

'What wisdom can you bring to bear on this situation? What is the truth of what has happened here, to your understanding?'

Parlòp shrugged. 'It was clear enough, Kelsari. Kalanomena was not dead. He created a copy of himself, a solidified phantasm of his own self. Then he killed it . . . him – or the copy killed him. We do not know which, for both are now dead.' She glanced over at Taraganam who was studiously looking away. 'There may not be a difference . . . Lord.'

The Kelsari ignored the gentle lack of respect she showed him. 'So why? If this was the act of a Karsara wize invading a relic of ancient Vyderbo, which is under our protection . . . if this is an internal matter among the Karsar wize, why are they moving their armies against us?'

This was clever – the situation he had placed her in. She stood before him and did not know what Taraganam and Krasne had reported to him. Had they told the truth or made up a strange and devious story to try to obscure it? She did not know. So she could, by her words, contradict what they had said.

But it did not matter. She was a mystic – truth and reality were what she sought. Mystics discovered and then taught. *This is our way.*

'With a crystal he found in the vaults of Vyderbo and by his magic, Kalanomena transported us to the tower of Turganamena.

It was his intent, I believe, to usurp the power of his lord. Instead, his lord killed him – this was the second time he died. Taraganam moved us from that place and, eventually, returned us to the vaults where you found us.'

Taraganam was now gazing at Parlòp but her emotions were unreadable. Parlòp hugged the staff to her chest and tried, by its power, to discern them. She sensed nothing but boredom. Did Taraganam despise these proceedings? Did she not care what Parlòp said?

'So, why move against us? The rebellion was one of his own. Yet his armies are coming hard. The vanguard will be with us in a day.' As if on cue, as the Kelsari spoke a riverguard entered and ran up to the Confluent. Parlòp heard a lot of whispering and then the guard left. For a moment everyone's attention was on this exchange and not what, if anything, Parlòp might say.

They were readying their troops for the attack. It wasn't surprising but she wondered what it meant for her and them all. She wondered where Krasne was. Had he returned to his family or had his duty sent him elsewhere again? She looked back at the Kelsari who was staring at her and not patiently, awaiting her response.

'He desires the crystal,' said Parlòp.

'Why? What powers does it give?'

He already knew this. Parlòp understood that. Krasne said he had reported it to the Confluent. There would be little doubt that the warlord and the Dawen would have passed it on to the king – even if Krasne himself had not told him.

'As Krasne reported to the warlord beside you,' she said, deciding she needed to cut through the charade, 'it has the power to make the phantasms of the wize real. Kalanomena made many horrors from his desires – and his imagination. This beast beside me was, we believe, a nightmare of his childhood.'

The shadow beast had been crouched on the floor beside her. If it could have made itself invisible it would have done. But at the mention of itself, it sensed something. It looked up at her and then gazed across the throne room to the Kelsari. After a few seconds, it rose from the floor to stand beside her, stretching to its full height, an icon of horror. Satisfyingly, Parlòp saw a stir amongst the nobles and guards.

'Is it safe?' said a supercilious-looking man standing near Taraganam. He moved back as he spoke. He did not introduce himself.

'It is . . . tamed.' Parlòp rather relished his reaction. 'It will do my bidding. All the beasts will when treated well by the Solpsar. This is our way.' She hoped, as always, that this did not reveal the sheer mastery of their magic. Let the Kelsar go on believing that the swamp people were merely animal trainers. The reality they must not know.

To make her point and, she hoped, gain some control of this interview she moved sideways and stood among the claws of the beast. It folded inwards and surrounded her with its body, stroking her shoulders with gentle claws. Feeling its affection for the one who had freed it, she gazed out from her new position and watched the wave of discomfort ripple across the Kelsar nobles.

Better.

The Confluent was whispering to the Kelsari. Nothing was said for a moment and then the Kelsari looked back at Parlòp. 'Why does Turganamena move against us, mystic? What else do you know of his intentions?'

Parlòp shrugged. This was becoming boring. 'I know nothing of his intentions, Lord Kelsari. But I am sure that he will not care what I or any of you know. He comes for the crystal.' She stretched herself.

'Wize Karsar Taraganam says she will defend us against his attack.' He glanced briefly at her as he said it.

'She believes she can,' said Parlòp. 'Perhaps it is true, but the cost of the magic she employs is too great. It should not be.'

'But it is,' said Taraganam harshly, speaking for the first time, cutting across the king.

'It need not be,' said Parlòp. 'We can forget this thing. Destroy it.'

'Show me its power,' said Chrasm.

'You asked this before,' said Taraganam testily. 'This is no parlour trick. My friend and colleague Kalanomena indulged himself too much. I will not use it for unbound desires or tawdry chicanery. I will use it for good. To make this world better.'

'Does that include defending this city and our riverland?'

'I have already said this. Must we go through it again now that the Solpsara is here? She too knows it.'

'You are a Karsara,' said the Confluent savagely. 'Why would you fight against your own people?'

Taraganam shook her head. 'I have said. I would make my home among you. Turganamena will not welcome me back to Karsar lands and none of the other towers can stand against him. He will mobilise them all against you. And I will not go to him. He killed a man I . . . admired. Kalanomena did not deserve such a death. His obsession drove him to insanity. He needed to be cared for, not assassinated by Turganamena's vile flesherer. I will fight to defend you . . . and you will give me a place in the riverlands.'

Parlòp stood silent through all these exchanges. She noticed wryly that Taraganam had not asked. She had told him. Clearly, the conversation had been had before, several times, but the Kelsari did not trust Taraganam. The only ones who really understood were Parlòp, Krasne and Taraganam – and Poxuul the makkuz. The Kelsari did not. And that was why she stood before the king.

Perhaps . . . ? This was hopeless. The politics were too complicated – there was no way out. There would be war. Had there ever been any doubt?

'Can I return to the swamp?' She snapped the words out more stridently than she intended. 'I would go to my temple. This is no concern of mine or my people. You summoned me to discover who killed Kalanomena to avert war. We know who killed him. He killed himself and then he attacked his own lord. Now there is still war between your peoples. It is nothing to the swamp.' The Kelsari was gazing at her with an uncompromising look. 'Release me,' she finished, feeling the harshness return to her voice.

'We may need you to carry a message to the Solpsari—' said the Dawen.

'You have other messengers. Send them.'

'You will stay,' said the Confluent roughly.

'We need your wisdom still,' said the Kelsari more gently. 'I would count it a boon if you stayed with us a little longer.' He smiled. 'I'm sure your king would agree.'

Parlòp sighed, exasperated. She did not speak but turned and placed her head in the chest of the shadow beast. It enveloped her in its claws. Parlòp heard a satisfyingly astonished gasp around the throne room. Her point was made. But she was unsure what her point was. She just wanted not to be there, not to be responsible, not to have been sent.

◊◊◊

The following day dawned, and it was beautiful. Parlòp had been welcomed back to the chambers where she was being ... held by her three sentries. She had slept on their ridiculously comfortable bed. She let the shadow sleep with her. They awoke together as the sun rose over the riverlands; its light filled her bedroom but she could not see the disc of the sun.

After her audience – or was it an interrogation? – there had been much more talking. More anger too, but Parlòp had quietly moved to the side of the room. The nobles and courtiers had hastily separated to let the fearsome shadow beast through. She had sat against the wall with it and waited for the arguments to be over. She had not listened to most of it. It did not matter. War was coming however much they talked about it. What else was there to say? The only worthwhile preparations, it seemed to her, were the preparations of the fighting men and women who would be manning the defences of Kel'Katoh. Parlòp commanded no troops – and would not wish to, even if they had been given. Her people only fought when they were threatened or directly attacked. They did not begin wars. After all, they desired nothing outside the swamp and its creatures.

Eventually, they had tired of talking or of her not listening and she had been welcomed back to her rooms, her prison.

In the light of the new day, Parlòp strolled onto the balcony. She looked out over the city. The river at this point flowed between rocky crags on either side, the cliff on the Karsar side being the highest. Just above the cliff, the land rose to the southern pass to the Kelsar lands beyond. If the Karsar had already taken the south then it was through this pass they would come.

She looked over at the cliff from the side of her balcony. At its top, the Kelsar had long ago built a wooden palisade to protect the pathways down to the river. Even when they breached the palisade the fight down to the city would be treacherous and intricate. It would not be an easy descent. If it were, the Karsar would have conquered Kel'Katoh before this. The southern lands often changed hands in the ebb and flow of Kelsar and Karsar wars. The capital had never fallen.

If the Karsar simply held the cliff and rained destruction down on the city, the Kelsar would break the city apart and scatter its pontoons and wherries. Another war would come to nothing. Wars never came to anything but death.

Several Kelsar men down in the street were pointing at her and sniggering. Annoyed, she realised that she had, without thinking, just risen as she always did, naked, ready to swim – as if she had been at home beside her temple. *Runneler men!* She returned to the room and donned her robe. The shadow beast was still sleeping, but as she pulled the robe down she saw that it was staring at her through one eye. A wary animal stare that said: What are you going to do next? Should I move?

But Parlòp did not know the answer. What should she do next?

She called the beast to follow and opened the door to her chambers. Surprised, she found there was only one sentry outside. He was standing but he was leaning against the wall, dozing. It was the age-old skill of the sentry – to sleep standing up. She crept by, hoping not to disturb him. He woke a little as the shadow beast passed him by, but he did not move. A few moments of them both standing still and he had slid back into a contented doze.

Parlòp slipped down the stairs to the ground floor of the palace. Servants were moving around but no one challenged her or stopped what they were doing to look at her, which was strange given the fearsome monster that accompanied her.

She stepped outside the palace through the great entrance doors. The guards on either side of the doorway let her pass without comment. Perhaps they knew who she was and that she was a guest of the Kelsari. Perhaps they did not realise her stay was a confinement. Perhaps they did not care.

She walked briskly around the palace towards the crags of Vyderbo. She reached the edge of the floating city, near where the Kelsari had been fishing that day. She found a point where the barricade was merely a wall just a little shorter than her. She looked over it at the water of the river, the slight waves bobbing. The tide was in. The city was high up the sides of the island of Vyderbo.

She wanted to leap the barricade and dive into the water, voicing the beast to follow. She looked longingly out over the river; she should escape to the swamp. There was nothing more she could contribute here.

Her temple home would be waiting for her. All the familiar animals in the swamp around her would greet the return of their Solpsara guardian. The Grandee and the Solpsari, the excellent, would understand that the river people did not want to listen to her. After all, they never did.

But, for some inexpressible reason, she didn't. Something stopped her, some nameless doubt, a feeling of a task unfulfilled. It was integrity. It was the need to do the right thing. That was what stopped her. There it was. She could not swim away and leave the world in this state. The crystal gem would break everything, just as it broke the people who wielded it. If it survived, everything would change – perhaps even the very nature of the people that lived in the world. And it would not be good.

Taraganam was mistaken. She would never be able to foresee the results of her actions. Her good intentions would not be enough to prevent her from doing evil with this thing. Her yearning to do good would lead her to choose the bad. Doing bad would just be an excuse – required to achieve good.

Parlòp found herself walking, heading further behind the palace to the walkways and eventually the stairs that led up the sides of Vyderbo itself. The beast followed her meekly, not even wondering where they were going, just content to follow, to be with her. She climbed back to the top of Vyderbo and slipped back into the ruins. She walked through them until she reached the southern edge of the crag. Across the river were the cliffs of the canyon's edge, and the palisade built to defend the paths. She sat down cross-legged on the very edge of Vyderbo and watched.

There were riverguards in Vyderbo, forming up, making preparations, building missile weapons. She knew that this place would be part of the preparations for war. The height of Vyderbo would make it ideal for batteries of missile weapons and squads of bowmen. As she sat, she was conscious of riverguards busy behind her. She sat there for a long time. What was her next move? She did not fancy her chances of stealing the crystal from Taraganam. The wize would be too quick, would confuse her with phantasms, real or imagined. Parlòp would fail and die.

'Everyone is looking for you.'

She turned. Krasne stood behind her. Whether he had arrived with one of the squads of guards or had been searching for her she did not know.

'I'm sure they are.' She looked back at the cliffside.

'The sentry is in trouble,' he said mildly, behind her.

Parlòp shrugged. 'He was asleep. I decided . . .' What had she decided? It did not feel like she'd made any choice. 'I needed to think,' she said eventually. She turned around and looked at him. 'What will happen now, Krasne?'

'War,' said the guard. 'First, there is always war.'

Parlòp looked back at the high cliff and the twin forts guarding the pass. On its very top, there was the glint of sunlight on armour, sword and shield. She sighed. She understood what it meant.

Turganamena had arrived.

Chapter 15

'Understanding was in the beginning.
Understanding was light
and life.
Darkness shall never overwhelm it.'

The Creation Song

The battle was unusual.

Parlòp watched it begin simply enough. Turganamena's vanguard of Karsar formed up, just below the height of the pass. She knew that gave them the advantage of higher ground. If the Kelsar attacked they would have to labour up the slope. If the Karsar came they would be charging down. She wondered why the Kelsar had not, in anticipation, taken the pass and its forts. Did they wish the Karsar to be there?

Parlòp saw no parley. No riders approached with the symbols of an envoy; there was no exchange of demands. Did either side see a compromise? Turganamena wanted the crystal. Two wize could not wield the crystal together. There was only victory. There would be one winner.

Ranks of Karsar archers formed up in front of the main body of their army. The first row shot flaming arrows at the wooden palisade defending the pathways down to the river. The brands thudded into the walls. The defenders moved quickly to douse the flames and as they did the second rank's volley of arrows caught them out of cover. They scurried back as yet more flame arrows from the reloaded first row thudded around them. A strange dance of attempted incineration continued for several rounds.

At last, the Kelsar missile troops responded. Catapults and ballista from behind the palisade fired back. The Karsar archers retreated – then quickly stepped forward to fire already nocked arrows and swiftly backed away again. The Karsar were faster and more expert in their attack than the defenders. These were seasoned troops. It was not surprising. Parlòp knew that the towers of the wize spent a lot of time fighting each other. Turganamena had united the towers. Very few wizards had achieved that in recent decades, if not a hundred years. His prowess with the wize magic and with military strategy was prodigious.

So the Solpsar had been happy that the riverlands lay between them and the wizard towers. Perhaps that was why the Solpsari, the excellent, had sent her to help avert a war that might result in a threat to the swamp. In that, she had manifestly failed.

The riverguards were forced into a mainly defensive position. They did their best to fire back but they were not winning. Even Parlòp could see that. Around her, the longer-range trebuchet and catapults on Vyderbo were ready to fire. The trebuchet, at the least, would reach the enemy, over the heads of the cliffside defenders. Was this why they had allowed the enemy to take the pass? Their range was great. They fired. Many of their first volley missiles fell a little short. Had the Karsar known this when they formed up where they did? Parlòp was no military strategist. She did not know. But once again, had the Karsar shown greater martial skill?

It was confusing, but the trebuchet had at least stopped the main body of troops advancing further. Their archers also were more reluctant to run and shoot at the defenders.

Is it a stalemate?

This situation certainly remained for some time. The Karsar troops were unenthusiastic to press their attack. That puzzled Parlòp. Her people fought only when attacked or when their lands were encroached upon. Yet surely the pause only gave the Kelsar more time to prepare a stouter defence.

Were they waiting for something?

The answer came when, in the late morning, the main army of the Karsar arrived over the pass. They brought with them a large number of war machines.

The Karsar set up these on the two flanks. The exchanges of missile fire increased in ferocity and frequency. But the Karsar catapults were nearer to the palisade of the Kelsar. Even more Kelsar guards now manned these defences. The wize did not need to strike the catapults on Vyderbo – they attacked the palisade.

A tactical error perhaps in placing the Kelsar artillery on the ancient crag. It gave better protection from attack, but they were further away. Her people had always thought Traizer, the warlord of the Kelsar, a ferocious and cunning general. Parlòp wondered if it were so. The warlike Karsar had surely outmanoeuvred him.

The Karsar catapults did great damage to the palisade of the cliffside defenders. Fire arrows from the archers swarmed down on them as well. It could not be long before the Karsar army charged the barricade on the clifftop.

Parlòp did not like fighting – even, if she was honest, in defence. So she had listened little to military strategies or ideas, even from her own people. But it seemed strange to her that there was as yet no sign of any phantasms. Often in a conflict between them, the wize would quickly utilise phantasms to confuse, to make the enemy unsure. Turganamena was said to be a master of this.

Yet she could see no sign of it – unless part of the whole Karsar army was a projection of a wize. It was possible. But the catapults and arrows were real. Riverguards were dying. Or they seem to be, she thought glumly. It could all be phantasy. That was surely unlikely.

But that was how confusion worked. She sighed.

She watched the increasingly one-sided battle, wondering if Turganamena would attempt to send the assassin through the lines. He could be made invisible by his magic, as she had seen. But would the killer make it through undiscovered?

The catapults of the Karsar army were, with their greater range and increasing accuracy, firing right over the defensive battlements. They did not reach Vyderbo but their missiles rained down on the pontoons and barges of southern Kel'Katoh. Parlòp, sitting on that side of Vyderbo, gazed down upon the panicking Kelsar. She felt sorry for the ordinary people and watched as they untied the ropes between the pontoons. The city was breaking. The city was scattering. *'A day to cast away, and a day to gather together.'* Krasne had quoted it, so long ago.

The Kelsar punted and paddled their homes away into the wider river, but other boats wended their way between the escaping barges. They bore yet more armed men – the Confluent had ordered more riverguards to the cliffs to reinforce the defence. She watched as they reached the cliff and tied their boats loosely. They climbed tortuous paths as ordinary people's homes were broken.

A rock from a Karsar trebuchet flew over her head to smash into a building behind her. With dismay, she realised it was only a matter of time before the catapults achieved Vyderbo's range. That time had come. She rose to her feet and called the beast to her side, then turned and gazed behind at the ancient ruin. It would only add to the destruction of the place. The Kelsar revered the place as a city of their ancestors, but this war would send it further into devastation.

And no one cares.

Parlòp retreated. She moved beyond the lines of guards and catapults. She saw Krasne, briefly, with a squad of soldiers. She kept walking until she found herself in the large city square of Vyderbo. This debacle had begun that day as she stood there with Taraganam and Caresma. Was that a century ago? They had come, puzzled over Kalanomena's death, tasked to discover the truth. Had they known what terrors were ahead of them, she would have run away.

She strolled over to the large tree that she had sensed on that day. She placed her hand on its trunk and felt again its concerns, its wonderful vegetative calm. The staff guided her deeper into its being. It was, in a way, aware of the activity around it. It was not concerned. It sensed no fire as there had been before. It did not detect a threat.

She allowed its peace to flood her, letting its surety of the continuation of its life give her the assurance she lacked, then slipped her hand away from the trunk and its sense of life faded. She wrapped both her hands around the staff and wondered when life would return to normal. What was normal anymore? She walked back to the square towards the strange arch. Her hand brushed the megalith's strange white stone, and she marvelled again that it was one of the few structures in Vyderbo still intact.

She stood next to one of the uprights and leant tiredly against it. She wondered about slithering to the ground but she did not. The shadow beast stood nervously beside her.

What bizarre noble impulse had made her stay? To see this whole catastrophe through to whatever conclusion? But the end was always war and death. What did she owe these people? She found nothing here that the swampers valued or yearned for.

She cared more for the animals who lived around her temple than she did for most people. She knew that. It was a truth she had been early in discovering about herself. People were difficult. Beasts were honest in their likes and their hatreds. They were what they were – violent and threatening or nervous and scared. You could never be sure of people. People lied. Beasts never did. Trees never did.

The shadow was trying its best to hide behind her, away from the sight of all the activity. Since the beast was larger than her it was a futile task. But still, it tried. She wondered if she should have left it where it had been created, in the vaults, all its world before she summoned it and led it out. Now there was even more danger.

She stood there for some minutes. She could no longer see Krasne – he must have been busy with his men. She waited.

Eventually, to her dismay, the Kelsari arrived with a large retinue. The Dawen Torgane was with him. Behind them at the back, as if reluctant, came Taraganam. It looked as if she had been forced to come – there were many riverguards. Perhaps they did not realise her power. She could no longer be forced to do anything.

The Dawen greeted Parlòp with obvious dissatisfaction. He muttered some words about wandering off. But the exchange was short. She did not reply and the minds of the Kelsar were not on her and her disobedience.

She stood and watched them as they formed up next to megalith.

The Kelsari spoke to Taraganam. 'So, will you conjure some reality to oppose their army?' He pointed to the cliff to the south, even though they all knew where the enemy was. Parlòp looked. The fighting was continuing. It looked like Turganamena's forces were readying a charge under the cover of their archers. Did they believe their catapult artillery fire had cowed the defender enough for them to break through?

Taraganam sighed. Her reluctance to act was palpable. Parlòp hugged the staff to her chest. The strength of the wize woman's emotions was disturbing. This was what Taraganam had offered the Kelsari. But she was still about to use the crystal against her own people. She might kill people she knew. This was the evil to be done to justify the good.

Taraganam walked slowly forward. She stopped a few feet from Parlòp and smiled briefly at her. 'Mystic, you will see the wonderful things I will do with this crystal.' She glanced over at the battle. 'But first I must deal with my lord. He will not stop his attack. There is no choice.'

Taraganam turned away and, without moving, looked over at

the cliffs. The gem was already in her hands, clenched in a tight, savage fist. She lifted it slowly.

Giant warriors dressed in furs and leather appeared on the top of the cliff. They had glimmered into existence right before the Karsar assembling for the charge. In form, they were ferocious Hardsar, an outlawed people who lived further to the west of the mountain range. There were only, perhaps, twenty of them. But they were no Hardsar. They were gigantic – three times the height of real hill bandits.

They had great axes. They stepped forward and swung them ferociously over their heads. The Karsar opposite them did not respond. Did they suppose them to be phantasms? Just the wild dreams of a wize, not worth running from because it was so obvious. Surely Turganamena knew what Taraganam held? He must know it could conjure the real. Otherwise, why attack? Had he not told his forces? Had Turganamena sent this army ahead and not explained what they faced?

This first of his army would be from the nearest of the towers. Had they come without proper understanding? Was Turganamena still to arrive? Perhaps he was further south. How could he be so callous as to send armies without them knowing what they faced?

For this was no subtle no phantasy of the wize. They faced their death.

Some wizard in the Karsar forces decided the giants worthy of a response. Massive winged lizards, like the chaos dragons of the creation myth, appeared in the air over the Karsar – a wize matching phantasy for phantasy.

Parlòp swallowed. *They do not understand.*

The giants charged, axes swinging. They reached the Karsar lines. They connected. Death spurted into the air – there were screams. The shock hit Parlòp like a physical thing. She pulled the staff away from her chest as the terrors of the dying swept into her. The sound and clash of battle filled the air. Was it she herself who died? She felt death. She felt despair. She felt their surprise. They were mortal. It was not another who would fall beside them this day. It was them. It was terrible. *'If a thousand fall beside you; if ten thousand die around you. The blade will not touch you.'* And then it did.

The Kelsari Chrasm, standing a few feet away, chuckled.

The giants did not pause. The Karsar phantasy dragons dived at the Kelsar lines but they roared away, unable to do any damage.

They were not real.

Parlòp sank slowly to the ground, a feeling of despair overcoming her. She was Solpsara. She was mystic. Her magic was the magic of life. This was not life. This was death. This was the good that Taraganam would do. The killing went on. More Karsar troops appeared over the pass, but panicked by the rout and the dying, they hesitated and then they too broke ranks and fled.

And no invisible assassin arrived to kill Taraganam. The Karsar had no way of discovering where Taraganam was. That was the mistake that Kalanomena had made. He had revealed himself. This crystal was best wielded by the bearer in secret – the power of hidden wickedness. Taraganam and the Kelsari stood many hundreds of feet away and doled out death, remote and uncaring. Was it not more honourable to face the person you must kill and who wanted to kill you? To know their name before you fought?

The Karsar retreated. Of Turganamena there was no sign.

The Kelsar troops remained in their defences. Indeed, more troops arrived by boat. Guards climbed the paths to reinforce.

The Kelsar defenders sent out a small patrol. Parlòp was not sure why – what did they scout for? Then she realised. They had been sent to kill the wounded Karsar. The giant hill bandits were at the summit of the pass. For a moment, they stood framed against the sky between the twin forts. They hesitated. Their job was complete.

The Kelsari stepped to Taraganam's side, slightly forward of her. 'Thank you. That was impressive.'

She turned to look at him. Her face was not sad. She was flushed and filled with the thrill of destruction. She was drunk on power. She laughed. And it was a crazy, demented laugh. Did madness come or had it already arrived? The Kelsari laughed gently back at her. And he smiled. She gazed back at him, unseeing, lost in the power she wielded.

The Dawen had stepped behind her. He drew a hasty dagger from his belt and thrust it, quite expertly, up through her back, severing her spine, and then further, into her heart. Gurgling amazement filled her throat. She collapsed, her face filled with the surprise of death. The Kelsari snatched the crystal from her loosened fingers before she hit the ground. Parlòp stared at the Dawen in horror. How did that fussy little man have such violence?

'Thank you for the demonstration . . . at last,' said the Kelsari to Taraganam's corpse. 'It was quite instructive.'

Chapter 16

'Find life and you find me.'

The teachings of the mystics

'Remove the carcass,' said the Kelsari and lifted the crystal to stare into its swirling depths of light and shadow. 'We need dialogue with the Karsar vixdeg no longer.'

'A wise move, lord.' The Dawen stood next to him, quietly cleaning his dagger with a buff-coloured cloth. 'You can never trust the Karsar. They are deceitful.'

Parlòp rose from the ground. She reached out and physically pulled the shadow beast closer to her. Why was she here? What was the point? The guards of the Kelsari's retinue came forward and lifted Taraganam's corpse from the ground. Blood dripped, uncaring, from the body as they raised her.

'We will enjoy working this wonder,' the Kelsari continued, ignoring her removal. 'The river people will be victorious.'

This was what Parlòp had feared. The crystal would destroy. The power was too much – to create everything and anything you craved. It would break all those who held it. And those it did not break would themselves break the world.

As if the Kelsari had heard her thoughts he turned and looked at her. 'Ah, Solpsara, we are pleased you have remained with us.' He smiled a thin, insincere smile. 'It is best that one who knows the power of this thing, and who now wields it, is the emissary we send to your Solpsari. You will return to your people. Then you will bring back their surrender. You will explain what little choice remains to Fleráp. Then we will be gracious and merciful. We will not send our phantastical forces against you. Your people will yield to our will, mystic. The Solpsar will join our new empire. We will join the swamper forces and your tamed animals to our army.'

He looked up at the cliff where the decimated Karsar army was being mopped up by his guards. The phantastic giant hill bandits stood at the height of the pass, unmoving as if they no longer knew what to do. 'We will march together against the Karsar.' The king's faint smile faded. 'It will be best for your people. You, of all swampers, know this.'

Such was the power of the emotions that assailed her, Parlòp considered ordering the shadow beast at her side to attack. The beast would certainly die. She would certainly die. Was that not preferable to slavery? The river people had desired for centuries to dominate river, tower and swamp. Now she would be the bearer of that doom. She would forever be the one who told her people that they were not free. They would be subject to the tyranny of the river. The cunning of the Solpsar, their knowledge of the swamp and the magic of life had always kept them free. That would all end. This brutish riverking would be their overlord. It could not be.

She leant forward, readying herself to die.

At that moment the Confluent Traizer arrived with a large retinue of guards. 'Majesty,' he said, stepping to the Kelsari's side without preamble. 'Ships have been spotted entering the river from the sea. There are more Karsar troops aboard – many more.' He looked concerned. 'They are already close, lord. We had diverted many troops here. We emptied the forts and villages at the mouth of the river. Our army was committed to the defence of the pass. I believe now that the first attack was a distraction.' He shook his head. 'They have already reached some of the wherries who scattered downriver from the southern city – the common people who had sculled downriver to escape the bombardment.'

The Kelsari laughed. The Confluent looked shocked and across his face passed doubt that the king had truly understood.

'Then we will be testing our new powers sooner than I thought,' said Chrasm. 'Confluent, we will go to the eastern end of Vyderbo. I will summon monsters of the deep ocean to destroy them.' He smiled at the warlord.

'Order the rest of the city to cast off,' said Torgane, the Dawen. 'They will not seize Kel'Katoh.'

'You worry too much, Dawen,' said the king. 'You always have.'

A Kelsara guard woman came to stand beside Parlòp and the shadow beast scurried away from her. Parlòp sensed a threat. Had she come to kill her? Instead, the woman leaned forward and spoke urgent words from the side of her mouth. 'You see the truth of it. Be ready to take whatever opportunity we can, mystic Parlòp. I have received word that my lord Raczek comes. When he arrives he will attack. He is not forbearing . . . like me. This will not end well for Kelsar or Solpsar. You see now that we must seize and destroy this crystal before it breaks your world. We makkuz are watchers. We do as little harm as we can. But sometimes we must act. Help me prevent a slaughter. I have come to favour my charges the Kelsar and the Solpsar as well. My lord is not as indulgent.'

Parlòp turned and stared into the strangely bland face of the riverguard. She had never seen her before. She was a Caresma thing – Poxuul the makkuz.

'I—' she began, but Poxuul had slipped quietly away.

Four guards appeared. They did not approach too close for fear of the shadow. 'Come,' they said. 'The Kelsari commands you to the eastern end of Vyderbo.'

The shadow beast rose to its full height. The guards took a hasty step backwards. Parlòp glanced at the beast and considered again whether to command an attack. They could attack. She could die. Yet, if she lived, there was still an opportunity to seize and somehow destroy the monstrous obscenity of the crystal. It still mattered not whether she trusted Poxuul. He was right. It was a power that must not be. If she sacrificed herself in anger, the gem would still break the world. Her vengeance was not worth the consequences. And the shadow would be dead. She forced her emotions down. Saimar had already died for his obedience to her. The shadow must not follow, even if it were to its death with her. The Solpsar did not just command the animals.

We care for them. Follow the riverking. See what he does.

She nodded to the guards and swung east, calling the shadow beast. Walking briskly ahead of them, she marched after the king. The shadow followed her meekly. He was still more scared of life itself than his appearance made people think. But its claws, its teeth, kept the riverguards from mistreating her. They did not come close.

The entourage of the king was ahead. By the time Parlòp arrived at the eastern edge of the rock they were gathered in the large ruin that housed the entrance to the vaults. She glanced at the steps down as she passed. Strange emotions assailed her. She would never enter that place again. Nothing would make her.

The Kelsari stood at the far end, where the cliff fell away to the river. Parlòp stood near the cliff edge to the side of him. She could already see several of the seagoing ships sculling up from the river mouth. Behind, others were furling their sails and troops were deploying the oars to row their way up the river. There were at least ten of them – all packed with Karsar.

As she watched, they broke formation and scattered across the width of the river. It was surely a strange tactic. They came in great random zigzags. Parlòp was no admiral. War was an affront to life. But shouldn't they come in a great phalanx? Was it some clever stratagem to avoid a concerted attack? It puzzled her.

She leant forward, looking over the edge at the river swirling below. The floating city, Kel'Katoh, the mouth of many rivers, was breaking apart, dispersing across the river before the new attack. Parlòp watched with stunned amazement at the sight of the many pontoons that made up the city being sculled and punted away towards the riverbanks or towards the streams and rivers that entered the main channel.

Yet more of the barges were being punted with large poles back up the river. They would have broken earlier, escaping the bombardments from the battle of the pass. They allowed or intended themselves to drift downriver towards the wide mouth. Then the invading ships had come. The leading Karsar ships would be on them soon. They were faster. It was a scene of chaos.

Parlòp held her breath.

The Kelsari lifted the gem and sniggered. Was that the same madness?

Five great leviathans, many-tentacled sea monsters, glowed into existence. They were behind the ships, where the sea and river joined. The Karsar were trapped. Parlòp could see no way out. The leviathans swam lazily towards the Karsar ships, gaining on them. They were powerful. They were fast. They could not be bested.

The Kelsari laughed. It was a maniacal laugh.

Parlòp had heard it before.

The Karsar ships were still zigzagging across the wide river. Some headed for the banks; others were intent on intercepting the pontoons that had made up the city. Parlòp found no hope in the tactic. The monsters would devour them all soon.

Many more ships appeared. They sprang into existence from nowhere, filling the river from edge to edge with Karsar ships. Phantasms – they had been conjured. Surely that would not work?

But such was the random chaotic motion of the real and the imagined ships zigzagging across the river, it quickly became impossible to tell which ships were real and which were imaginary. The sea monsters reached the Karsar at the rear. They attacked ferociously, throwing themselves at the ships. Of the five leviathans, only one hit a real ship, breaking it apart, throwing its troops and sailors into the river. The four other monsters collapsed through phantasms into nothing. Parlòp understood.

She saw another glimmer. Yet more ships came into existence, weaving and zigzagging, some forwards, some backwards, some heading for the cliffs at the sides of the river. The whole river was full of ships, phantasms, real and unknown. They passed through each other. It was now impossible to tell what was the truth and what was a conjuring of the wize.

Ships of the Karsar vanguard were now well among the scattering barges. Troops leapt from ships onto the pontoons of the city. Citizens threw themselves into the river to escape the soldiers; others tried to mount a defence. Were some of the attackers phantastical? Was the whole thing? Parlòp did not know. But, she knew somewhere in it all, real Karsar were killing real Kelsar. She just didn't know where. The Karsar moved on, leaping from barge to barge. Some they seized and punted towards the rock of Vyderbo.

The sea monsters were not finding the real ships. More Karsar had disembarked and were fighting their way through the scattering city. This attack was not going to be as easy to stop. The Karsar had again shown their greater mastery in battle. Their strategy was very clever. They were winning. Just as the Confluent had said, the whole attack at the pass had been a distraction – a way of diverting the Kelsar forces to the defence and away from the city.

Still the leviathans were attacking. But all the ships they attacked were imaginary. They found the real ones less and less often. Had the real ones already reached the city? The Karsar troops were seizing more of the pontoons of the scattering city. The Kelsari could not, surely, send his leviathans to attack his own city. They would reach Vyderbo. Were they already there?

Parlòp looked away from the chaos of the phantastical and glanced over at the Kelsari. On his face there was doubt and uncertainty. He was realising that this was more difficult than he had thought. This was the moment for her to run. She should escape and tell the Solpsari of the ultimatum. She should warn her people.

They should be ready for the coming war. Whoever won would turn next on her people. Whoever that was, Kelsar or Karsar, was unimportant. Parlòp backed away from the edge. There was nothing she could do. What noble hope had there ever been? Physically pulling the shadow beast with her, she hurried past the entrance to the vaults, through the guards all gaping incredulously at the terrible battle of the real versus the imagined. No one stopped her. No one cared where the swamper and her dark monster went next. She reached the roadway beyond and heard a commotion in the ruins ahead of her. She knew it was fighting – she had left it too late. The Karsar had reached Vyderbo. They had moved from barge to barge and rushed up the steps from the river city. They were fighting their way through the ruins. Did they know the Kelsari was here?

Parlòp hesitated. She did not want to run into a confrontation.

Was there time to get to the northern edge of the ruins and dive from them? She was an excellent diver but it was an extremely long drop. She hesitated. Even a swimmer of her skill might not survive. And what would be in the water beneath her? There would be barges, wherries and attackers. She would not know if they were real or imaginary. One would kill her. The other would set her free. She took a few steps in that direction and then doubted.

The sound of battle was closer. Too many of the Kelsar troops had gone with the king – they were all gathered at the eastern end. The guards remaining in the west of the ruins could not stop the attackers. Troops from behind her, from the Kelsari's retinue, ran past her, heading into Vyderbo to join the skirmish. Krasne appeared from the ruins ahead. He was running backwards, leading a band of guards desperately fighting a rearguard, some wounded, many blood-spattered, but whether with their own blood Parlòp could not tell. Krasne ran up to her, his face smeared with sweat and blood.

'Where is the Kelsari?' he demanded.

Parlòp pointed wordlessly to the far side of the ruined building. He ran. She turned back to follow him but stopped. She did not want to die with these river people. She had left it too late to dive. There was nothing left but to see this through. Krasne and his men had disappeared into the mass of riverguards forming up to protect their king.

Parlòp decided. She ran after Krasne. She reached the entrance to the vaults and wondered, briefly, if she should retreat into them for safety. But she could not do it. Her legs would not move, would not take her down those steps again. If there was no safer place than the vault left, they were all doomed. The Karsar would be there soon. She turned and ran again after Krasne, the shadow beast skittering and mewling beside her. Whatever was going to happen would encompass them all – and soon enough.

◊◊◊

She reached the line of Kelsar guards that had formed around the king. The Kelsari had turned from the river battle. It was lost and he knew it. He had abandoned the sea monsters to do whatever their nature demanded. He would defend himself and Vyderbo against the attack of the Karsar with some new conjuring.

Parlòp stepped to the line of troops. Thankfully the Kelsar let her through. Finding Krasne and his riverguard behind the line, she went and stood next to them. The beast skittered beside her.

But the attack of the Karsar did not come.

They did not press the advantage. They formed up on the far side of the ruined building in which they all stood, further than a bowshot away. It was as if an attack had never been their aim. Was this just containment? Why would that be? Did they fear the Kelsari?

The troops around Parlòp settled into a tighter defensive line.

Giant Hardsar warriors, the same as Taraganam had conjured, appeared in front of them. They strode towards the Karsar and swung great axes.

The Karsar broke into a skirmish line, not trying to mount a defensive front. The river people reacted, some guards breaking forward to pursue. Was it victory? They were ordered back.

Parlòp hugged the staff. At once she felt something strange. People were walking – no, creeping. Everyone she saw was running. But these were very stealthy. They were hidden. She felt their emotions of caution and wariness. This was no guard or Karsar invader fighting a wholesale battle. These were people with another objective.

To not be . . . seen. To find . . .

Parlòp swore. She remembered the invisible assassin who had killed Kalanomena. She swung around, looking back towards the Kelsari. Should she warn him? Would he have mercy on her people if she did? The king was utterly intent on the battles of his conjured hill bandits still pursuing the Karsar through the ruins. The passing presence faded. Cautious or not, they were moving fast. She stepped quickly away from Krasne – the shadow beast beside her squeaked in alarm – and headed towards the Kelsari.

There was a scream. A dagger was protruding from the Kelsari's chest. The assassin appeared beside him, laughing. He turned and struck the Dawen with the dagger in his other hand – up through one eye into the brain. Turganamena flickered into existence beside him. Their conjured invisibility was gone.

The Kelsari fell, the crystal bursting from his upraised hands and jerking rapidly forwards. It rolled onto the ground. There was her opportunity. Parlòp threw herself forward.

Turganamena seized the crystal from the ground before she reached it. He looked up, fixing her with an arrogant gaze.

Chapter 17

*'Our speech has the power of life and death,
and those who adore it
will eat its fruit.'*

The teaching of the mystics.

Parlòp stepped forward, unable to stop herself from getting closer, but she realised the threat behind the eyes of the wizard. She stopped. The shadow beast stretched up beside her, snarling and showing its claws. It knew there was a threat; it would attack. She ordered it to cease, grabbed and pulled it away from the wizard. It stared at her in confusion.

Turganamena's gaze broke. He turned the crystal over in his hand, then waved it before him. The Hardsar giants attacking his forces disappeared. Three giant Karsar soldiers appeared next to him, holding flaming swords.

Turganamena and his assassin were surrounded by Kelsar guards – but none of them moved. They stood and gazed at this wizard who was able to destroy them with a wave of his hand. Silently, his assassin walked over and stood beside his lord.

'You will all surrender to my men at once,' said Turganamena. 'Who is in charge?'

'The Confluent, Traizer . . .,' said a single guard, and then hesitated as Turganamena turned his gaze upon him.

'And where is he?'

Parlòp looked around. The warlord was nowhere to be seen. Had he gone forward to fight with his men against the encroaching Karsar? Was he even now mounting some sort of counterattack? Had he even come with them to the ruins?

The Karsar troops who had attacked them moved in. They came between the ranks of Kelsar guards and quietly disarmed them.

Any who resisted were bound or killed. Parlòp saw at least three Kelsar guards who did not come quietly enough die quickly and efficiently under the Karsar violence.

Much to Parlòp's surprise, Krasne appeared, stepping through the guards to stand before the wizard. 'Lord—'

Turganamena raised his hand, stopping Krasne in mid-sentence. 'You were in my tower.' His gaze swung to Parlòp. 'With this swamper and her monster. You were there with the traitor Kalanomena.' He glared at them both. 'Tell me why I shouldn't kill you instantly.'

'Lord, we were ... transported there by Kalanomena from the vaults beneath. It was there he found the crystal.' Krasne wore a look of resignation. Did he face his death? 'We did not attack your tower willingly.' It sounded despairing.

Turganamena turned the crystal over in his hands as if seeing it for the first time. 'Kala had propounded the existence ... his hypothesis of such a device of the ancients many times. There were stories of a great sorcerer at En'Hass, long ago. It was an obsession with him. Few believed him to be anything other than deranged on the subject.' He grunted to himself. 'Who knew he was correct. It was not until he appeared that I realised why he had petitioned to be the envoy to the Kelsar.' He looked down at the body of the king. 'Hardly necessary now – the riverlands will be added to our own. The first of many.'

Turganamena looked up again, leaving his musings to fix Krasne with his stare. The wizard did not speak. Krasne waited patiently. The Kelsar guards shifted nervously. This Karsar wizard could strike them down in a moment.

Turganamena turned his attention to Parlòp. 'And what is your purpose here, Solpsara? The river and swamp are hardly friends.'

'I was sent here. The Kelsari made a ... request of my king. He wanted someone to investigate the death of Kalanomena. I am mystic. We seek understanding.'

'The death of Kalanomena?'

Parlòp sighed and explained everything to the wizard – the duplicate Kalanomena, the journey through the vaults. The wizard listened silently, not interrupting or demanding clarification. He merely nodded as various events were relayed. Perhaps he knew that as a Solpsara mystic she was bound to teach, to relay the truth as she found it. Perhaps, strangely, he trusted her to tell him what occurred without bias – for she was mystic and, importantly, not of the river. If so, this Karsar had more respect for a Solpsara than any Kelsar – except Krasne.

Turganamena looked down again at the crystal. 'Making a copy of yourself – interesting concept. And travel at will . . .' He stopped.

'And where is Taraganam? She was Kalanomena's aide in the embassy and his long-term confidant. She even listened to his obsessive diatribes with patience. Where is she?'

'She was killed by the Kelsari.' Parlòp spoke intentionally brusquely. 'She held the crystal. He desired it.' The arrogance of the wize knew no bounds. Why should she disguise it?

The wizard shrugged. 'Well, for that alone, Chrasm's life would be forfeit.' He glanced down at the bodies of the king and the Dawen, then motioned to the Karsar troops. 'Come. Throw these cadavers off this rock. They deserve nothing.'

It looked for a moment as if some of the Kelsar present would object. In the end, their fear and doubt won and nothing was said. All knew that their objection would lead to more death – theirs. The Karsar came forward. They coerced some of the riverguard to carry the bodies of the riverking and his Dawen. They heaved them aloft and headed for the southern side of the crag. Parlòp lost sight of them amongst the ruins.

Turganamena turned to the assassin at his side. 'Take men and find the warlord Traizer. Bring him to me, or report back why you cannot. I will be in my new palace.' He guffawed. 'Once we find out where, in their panic, the Kelsar have punted it off to.'

He gestured harshly at Parlòp and then at Krasne. 'You two will come. I would understand more where this device was found. Perhaps there are yet more treasures of the ancients there.'

Parlòp did not speak. She walked after the Karsar wize. Around her followed Karsar troops and Kelsar prisoners. Turganamena could find out for himself the dangers that Kalanomena had conjured in that place. She had no intention of ever entering it again. The wizard strode imperiously past her. She watched him go and hugged the staff to her chest. If she was lucky, no one would remember that she had not arrived bearing the staff. No one cared enough about a swamper to notice. Anyway, she would claim it had always been hers. She had no intention of admitting that she had found a staff and that it was a device of the ancients.

She felt a momentary fear about the other staff that had been there. This one had amplified her magic. Was it for the life-magic alone? Or would it, in the hands of others, perform the same function whatever magic they wielded? What would this staff be capable of in the hands of a wize – or one of the other sorcerers that, people said, still wandered the world? The thought was perturbing.

Yet she did not relish going back into the vaults to retrieve it.

◊◊◊

She spotted the birds when they reached the square in the middle of Vyderbo. They were far off. Parlòp did not know why she noticed them, but she was not alone. Several of the Karsar troops saw them too and indicated to their lord.

Parlòp looked up, narrowing her eyes to see better. She understood then why she had noticed them. This flock of birds was unusual. They looked like zagles. But she had never seen zagles fly in groups of more than two, mated pairs. At least twenty zagles were flying towards them, arrow-straight. And there were, she realised, other birds with them. Hiwka? Kastra? It was strange. What was this?

She raised the staff but she could not sense birds. She could not feel in them the vigour of a bird, the power of their emotions, the strength of their wings. It was almost as if it was a flock of people flying towards her. Were they too far off? She realised what the emotions reminded her of. These weren't people. They weren't birds. There was arrogance, a confidence in who they were and how superior they were. It reminded her of Caresma, of Poxuul, and the feelings she had got from him when the staff was in her hands.

She stopped. That was it.

Poxuul's lord had come – Raczek, he had called him.

She swore under her breath and considered retreating. But she could not. Her curiosity as mystic got the better of her. Karsar, Kelsar and Solpsar she understood. Here was the chance to see the makkuz, the mythical nemeses of the ancient world – stories she had hardly believed. The enemies of legend were coming. She would see the makkuz lord. She would know the truth. What would happen?

Turganamena had stopped and was raising his hand. Would he strike the birds from the sky before they reached them?

With the crystal in their possession the only limit to the power of the wize was their imagination. Perhaps Kalanomena, Taraganam and the Kelsari had not been adventurous enough. She did not think this wize lord would suffer from the same limitations.

A Karsar guard Parlòp had not seen before stepped beside Turganamena. 'You would be wise not to stand against my lord.'

The Karsar lord turned an angry gaze on the soldier, his attention distracted from the birds. 'And who are you to question—'

There was a flash of fire and the soldier was replaced by the form of Caresma. He reached out his hand and fire burst from it. Turganamena jerked his hand back from the flame. Even so his flesh was burnt.

'Caresma—' he screamed. 'How dare you.'

Caresma stepped closer. 'I am not Caresma. I never have been. I am Poxuul. I am a thybuk planetary agent. I am makkuz. You will give me the gem now. I had hoped to do this quietly.' He glanced, meaningfully but briefly, at Parlòp. 'It is not our intention nor ever our aim to be seen. But this device cannot be allowed in the hands of primitives such as yourselves. We have had to save you once—'

Turganamena moved quickly. Brandishing the gem he turned to face the Caresma thing. He lifted his hand and Poxuul instantly responded with a ball of heat. Parlòp felt its intensity burning her face even from where she stood.

Turganamena fell to the floor screaming. His whole arm was blackened and burnt – she saw the whiteness of his bones showing through. The wize was already unconscious in shock. He lay inert.

'It is regrettable it has come to this,' said Poxuul. 'I liked your people. I did not wish for it. But my lord Raczek must not see that I was too cautious. He might report my failure to Lord Romul.' He bent down and took the gem from Turganamena's charred hand. The wizard did not move.

Nobody moved.

The flock of zagles, hiwka, kestra and felca arrived. They swooped down into the square. As they reached the ground they transformed into men and women. Their bodies shone as if in their very being there was a source of light and power.

Their leader, for he must surely be, was a rough-looking man whose being radiated ferocity and arrogance. 'So, Poxuul, your clandestine attempts to recover the device failed, I see. You have revealed yourself.' He scowled. 'You should have acted sooner, thybuk.'

Poxuul raised the crystal. 'Yes, Lord Raczek. You were wise, as you always are. But look, the quintessence crystal is here. We can destroy it. We can depart.'

Raczek gazed around the assembled crowd of Karsar and Kelsar. Everyone stared back at him with mixed looks of incredulity, fear and shock. Raczek's expression was mild as if he was almost entertained by their presence. His attention turned briefly to the other shining makkuz surrounding him.

'Kill them all,' he said calmly. 'They know of our existence. They have seen too much.'

'No, lord.' Poxuul screamed the words. 'I can destroy this and we can depart. These people are innocent.'

Raczek's attention turned back to Poxuul. He gazed at him for a few moments. None of the other makkuz moved. 'So you have gone native, Poxuul. I long suspected this of you. You lived too long amongst the primitives. You care about them. They are all dispensable to the greater good of the universe. And now they know. Stories of our existence must not arise. Kill everyone who has seen us. We will keep the device. It may be useful.'

In the next breath, his fellow makkuz shot balls and spears of fire out from their hands. Kelsar and Karsar together fell screaming, their whole bodies instantly blackened in the heat.

'No—' shouted Poxuul. 'I can destroy it. We can leave.' He raised the gem and, visibly gathering his strength, an incandescent ball of fire enveloped the hand that clutched the crystal. The fire cocooned the crystal in a miniature sun.

Darkness sprang into existence in the core of the small sun with a low whump. It streamed out, chasing the light outwards – a globe of shadow burst outwards. A sun of darkness was born, which ate the sun of light. The blackness engulfed Poxuul. With another massive thud, the darkness exploded outward. The makkuz stopped killing and scattered back.

Could the darkness hurt them? Could it kill them?

Parlòp did not know why but she ran forwards into the blackness. The shadow beast screamed its exultation and ran with her. She felt its gentle claws grazing her back. She felt its glee. She felt its joy. The darkness surrounded them.

Her world ceased to be.

Before her, in the blackness that was the whole of her existence, she saw a glimmer of light. She leapt for it, falling to the ground. Her hand closed around the crystal. She raised it. Its centre still swirled with light and dark, but she was surrounded by darkness.

She turned. Was this way north? Running from the sheer memory of where she had been, she burst from the darkness. It covered the whole of the square of Vyderbo. She found herself beside the ancient tree next to the square but did not stop. She ordered the shadow to follow – it was already beside her. She hurdled through the ruins, running as fast as her legs could go, leaping over walls and broken rocks. She did not look back. More screams sounded. The emotions of the dying swept into her through the staff. The makkuz were killing. Were they dying too? She ran. The dying were far behind her as she came to the edge of Vyderbo. A cliff edge yawned before her but she did not hesitate. She ordered the beast to follow and ran over the precipice without stopping. She swung her whole body round into a dive.

She looked down. Below were scattered pontoons and wherries of the broken city. But she was going to hit open water. She straightened, pulling the staff and the gem close to her body. She hit the water. The beast smashed into the river with all the grace of a rock.

She ordered it down, underwater, beneath the surrounding wherries. She turned herself underwater and pulled the robe from her body, rolling, expertly releasing and seizing the staff again. She swam.

The swamp. She must reach the swamp.

Chapter 18

*'Beneath the moving circle of fire
the living surface wakes and trembles
and once again begins a fearful travail.'*

From the song of suffering.

She worried during the trip home. Did they suspect her? Did they pursue her? She did not know. The worry consumed her. Parlòp stopped and searched the rivers behind her with concern. She hugged the staff to her but sensed no people, no pursuers.

It was a long journey from the broken city to her temple. She neared it after nearly two days of watchful, slow travel through the swamp. She had a lot of time to fret. But once she was in the waters near her home and the swamp was around her, she felt her distress lessen. She was back. She paused where Saimar had lived, where he had hunted and dwelt in peace until the day she had, once again, summoned him to her. She gazed at his familiar hunting grounds. She lay in the water holding the staff level with the surface and thought of him and the life he would still have if she had not taken him with her to the floating city. But her Grandee had ordered her to go. The Solpsari, the excellent one, had commanded it. She could not have gone alone. She thought perhaps even Saimar would not have wanted that. He would have wanted to be with her – to protect the one who protected him. The one who kept his swamp safe for him to hunt in, safe for him to dwell in. He had been an allarg and his nature and his intelligence were that of an allarg. But she had trouble believing that he hadn't, in his way, cared for her.

She stayed there, silently treading water and thinking of him for several hours. She cried. She hugged the staff and she hugged the shadow, who sensed her upset and knew her pain – for it was pain.

She let herself slip silently away towards the temple. The shadow beast did not like the water. It was not its nature. It was not made for swimming nor to live within such a place as the swamp. It wasn't made for anything or anywhere. It was the nightmare of a child that had escaped from his terrors. It was never meant to live. She still didn't know why it lived, or how it survived. It did not eat. It had no throat.

But it ran and swam with her. It would be on solid ground as much as it could, but the chance of losing her overcame its dislike of being in the water. She waited for it and it came with her. It was a little less afraid now. It knew her. It trusted her. It knew she cared. It preferred this place, where she was, and the other animals. It preferred a world without people, without Kelsar or Karsar – without wize, without the ambitions of lords and kings.

She did not rush anymore. It was more important to bring the beast home safely. Anyway, she was not sure. They might be waiting for her if they had worked out what she had done – worked out who now held the quintessence crystal. That was what Poxuul had called it.

She reached her temple. It was not changed and there was no one there. She made a slow circuit around it and greeted the animals with a gentle and relaxed voice. They responded as animals would – as if she had been gone just a few minutes. To each she sent an individual greeting and, as much as she could, showed them the shadow beast and let them come to terms with the arrival of an unknown creature, one that might usurp their food or their place. She tried to help them understand.

She waited patiently while they got used to the idea. Her staff was useful in this for the power now behind her voice was stunning even to her. And she understood their being, their lives so much better than she ever had before. With the staff, she felt like a blind person who had not realised they were blind until they could see.

When the swamp creatures were happy, or as happy as she could make them, she stood up. Then, flowing like the water, she slid lithely up to her temple. The beast came with her, curious. It sensed, she thought, the power of this bower for life. She walked to the central trunk – the tree that held and supported her temple. She stroked its bark and let herself feel its familiar vegetative life. She asked it, gently, to open. It was hesitant. It did not like to expose itself to the outside. The bark protected it. The bark was strong. But it did as she bid. It creaked open, one small hole in its very centre and a long slit, at her further bidding, along the main branch.

She took the crystal from her wet-leather pack and dropped it into the centre of the hole. The bark closed over it. She slid her staff into the branch and let the tree close its wood around it. She sent a gentle calming to the tree. She thanked it. Trees could not comprehend the voice, nor the summoning, but they could feel the order and the understanding. They were. They existed.

She was safer. They were safer.

If they came they would not find anything. Even another Solpsara mystic would not immediately think what she had done – at least not without much reflection. The tree would not tell them. The central tree of a temple was a hallowed thing. Once it had given the swamp the structure of the temple it was left alone in gratitude for its assistance. To do as she had done was close to irreverence. But she had to.

She settled and prepared herself some food. She had not eaten much on the journey home. There had been berries and leaves but nothing else. She was hungry. She tried to understand from the beast what sustenance it needed to survive, what it would need to live. But it did not seem to contain the concept of eating anywhere in its mind. It did not know the answer any more than she. It did not know what food was.

She was worried about that, but she could do little but eat herself. Perhaps the beast would eventually work out what it needed and request it. Perhaps it would understand nourishment by her example.

For the next two days, she busied herself with her life as a mystic of the swamp, studying, trying to decide how to teach the people she cared for locally. The village for whom she was mystic. She did not go there, for she was unsure what to say to her Grandee. She would have to lie to him and that was not the function nor the tradition of a mystic. But there was little choice. He must not know what she protected.

She hoped no one would ever come for the gem. She hoped that she could live out her span without ever seeing it again. When she was gone the tree would go on safeguarding it for much longer than she ever could. And when the tree eventually perished it would slip away with the tree, rotting into the swamp. With good fortune, it would never be found and would be forever lost in the dark alluvium of the river. As centuries passed it would be lost down the rivers to the ocean and vanish forever.

◊◊◊

The Solpsari, the excellent, arrived the following day.

He came with her Grandee, Tarbap. The creatures around her warned her of their coming long before they reached the temple. She summoned the shadow beast and ordered it to hide, quietly, on the far side of the temple. It was concerned. She calmed it and assured it that they did not come to threaten, but that they might be worried by its appearance. She was not sure it understood, but it hid in the darkest corner of the bower, a shadow lost in shadows.

The Grandee Tarbap came from the water first. He was an old man now but his body was strong and muscled. He would be her Grandee for many years yet.

'I greet thee, Grandee of mine. May your life be forever,' she said.

He bowed to her. 'I honour thee, mystic of the people. The king, the excellent, is come. He wishes to meet with you.'

She turned her head. The Solpsari, Fleráp, heaved himself from the swamp without further introduction. She bowed deeply to him.

'I honour thee, excellent one, Swamp king to the people of life.'

Fleráp was a much younger man than the Grandee, although he had been king for nearly ten years. His father had been lost in battle with the river people. Misled by a phantasm, he had been tricked into an ambush.

Fleráp was a cautious man. This king had made peace with those who had killed his sire. To do so would have been hard, she was sure. But he had done it – for the good of the swamp and the good of the people.

It was always his way to placate the Kelsar if he could. Perhaps the Solpsari, the excellent, appeased too much. War was always evil but it was, sadly, sometimes needed. It was why he had agreed to her going to Kel'Katoh. He had, she had thought, allowed himself to be outmanoeuvred by the wiles of the Kelsari. But now Chrasm was dead.

'May we consult with you, mystic Parlòp?'

'Of course, my lord and king, how may I aid you?'

'You were sent at our command to the floating city. And you have returned. Yet we have not had a report from you.' He paused, his mild censure spoken. He looked up. 'We have heard something of what happened there from others. But you did not come to us to tell us this . . .'

She bowed. Perhaps she should have gone to the village and seen her Grandee as soon as she came back. Now they suspected her of some falsehood.

'My sincerest apologies, excellent one. I meant no disrespect. I wished to bring the shadow beast home first.' She indicated it with a motion of the hand. It rose from the shadows and considered the Solpsari, mewling worriedly. 'It is very frightened, scared even of its existence.' It gazed balefully across at the king. 'It was created by a vile sorcery of the wize. It is not a natural animal. It deserves life though, as we all do. But it would not, could not go somewhere with many people it did not know.' She paused. 'Even so, I should have come before you. But there was no urgent danger.' She smiled what she hoped was a sincere smile. 'The floating city has scattered to save itself. Their king is dead. The chief wize, the Fount Caresma is dead. The Dawen is dead. The Karsar wizard Turganamena is dead. It will take the river and the towers many weeks, if not months to recover.'

The king nodded sagely. 'Yes, this I know. Chrasm has perished and the Confluent Traizer has made himself Kelsari. He, who has often turned his armies on the swamp. But his attention is presently on other things. He has banned the wize order in the riverlands. His edict says it is responsible for the terrors that assailed Kel'Katoh. And he prepares his forces for an attack on the towers for their leader is dead.' He paused, sighed, and fixed Parlòp with a stare. 'I understand, mystic Parlòp, that they fell upon a great marvel in the ruins of Vyderbo where the Karsara wize died – the man of whose murder you were sent to discover the truth.'

Parlòp gently shook her head. 'He was not murdered, my king – or, at least, he simply murdered himself. He created another form of himself using the vile arts of the wize and poured, so he said, all that was wrong of himself into it – the cowardly, the foolish and unhappy. Then he murdered his duplicate. His shadow-ka they called it, the wize who accompanied me.'

'So the Kelsar were innocent of the death. Yet the war was not averted between Kelsar and Karsar. Their city was scattered. And they blame the wize. And the . . . object that they found.'

Parlòp drew in a tired breath. 'Perhaps, my lord, there were many deaths in the end. I cannot say who will blame who. There was a madness that overtook them, I think. They, like Kalanomena, destroyed themselves in the end – with their greed and ambition.' She paused. 'We should keep out of it as best we can, my king. The swamp is for life.'

The Solpsari moved uncomfortably. Even without the staff, she sensed the change in him. Now he would come to the point, the real reason for his journey to her. He cared only in passing for the death of a Kelsari and a Karsar wize – if they did not involve the swamp. This now was the truth.

'How, then, did they create real forms that battled over Vyderbo and Kel-Katoh? How could he make the phantasms of the wize real and kill himself and each other? The magic of the wize has always been in trickery and phantoms. They use their arts to mask their true aims and actions. Surely they cannot create reality from nothing?'

Parlòp swallowed. She must lie. *How can I be a true mystic and lie?*

'It was no marvel, lord king. They used some vile engine to accomplish it, lord. I do not know the truth of it and, even though I am mystic and strive always for truth – I did not want to understand the foul arts of that blighted people. Perhaps another mystic would have been better suited to go. I do not wish to understand such a corruption of life.'

Her Grandee, Tarbap, spoke. 'Yet it was a thing of great power.' In his wiser eyes she saw something, a doubt, a feeling that his mystic was not speaking as all of her calling did – the truth as they knew it. 'Could we not have used it also? To defend the people against the machinations of the river?'

Parlòp shrugged, feeling even herself the falseness of the action. She shook her head. 'It was some foul machine of theirs, lord, wholly of their arts. I think . . . they thought it was some device of the ancient times, from the magician kings of old.'

'Can you know we could not have used it . . . and for good?'

And there it is, thought Parlòp. The same ambition that had killed them all. 'Perhaps we could, lord. But it was destroyed in the final devastation when the Fount of the Wize ... he was not of this world, lord. He was a makkuz, the foe of ancient times. A watcher, he called himself. He said we should not be allowed to possess it. That we could not be ... permitted to do so. He disappeared. His lord and his people, the makkuz, came. After the battle, he took it when he transformed himself to the true form of the makkuz – fire and heat.' She shook her head. 'It was then that I ran. I threw myself off the heights of Vyderbo into the river and escaped with the shadow beast. We will never know if the engine could be a device for the swamp, a power of life.' She looked up and fixed the Solpsari with a disrespectful stare. 'But it is my belief it was wholly of their corrupt art. It was wrong in itself.' She paused. Nothing was wrong in itself. She knew that. *It is just what people do.*

'So it is lost, even to us,' said her Grandee.

'If it is not,' she said, 'I do not know where it lies now. I think the makkuz took it. I think he destroyed it, as he vowed to do.' She had done it, the direct and the absolute disavowal of all that it was to be a mystic. She had lied.

The king gazed at her for several moments. 'And this is the truth you know, mystic Parlòp of Grandee Tarbap.'

'It is, lord king.' The shadow beast growled its accompaniment.

They looked over at the shadow. It had risen to its full height, gazing at them balefully.

They tried a little longer to get what they must have suspected was the truth. She did not waver. She remained unsure that she had convinced them. But perhaps they just hoped she had brought something of great power back to her people. But whatever evil there had been in Kalanomena, in Taraganam, in Chrasm, Poxuul the makkuz had been right. This device was not for her world in this age. It was not for the river or the towers of the wize. It must not be for the swamp. The device was too powerful.

She gave them food, as was the custom when visitors came. They slipped away as the day was moving to its end. The king, the excellent, looked back at her as he swam away, his gaze doleful. Her Grandee did not turn his head. She had disappointed him.

Parlòp went to the shadow beast and held it tightly until night fell. She did not sleep that night. *Will the nightmare never end?*

Epilogue

'All life you have given me, to protect and sustain.'

The teachings of the Grand Mystic.

The stranger came without warning.

He arrived the day after her Solpsari and Grandee left, on the riverbank nearest to Parlòp's temple. She had not seen him approach. None of the animals that lived around the temple had warned her of his coming. That was odd. They had warned her when the Solpsari came. Why not now? A jaksar had come with him. It was odd to see one in the swamp.

The stranger did not speak but dropped and waded into the swamp to cross the water between the bank and the temple in which she dwelt. He carried a simple staff and used it ably to steady himself, his robe floating and swaying around him. The jaksar did not follow him into the water but sat looking disdainful of the very idea of swamps and water. The forest animal watched the stranger wading through the river and yawned with boredom.

Parlòp did not move. The shadow beast, so skittish when any approached, worried even when the Grandee and the Solpsari had come, did not hide. It went and sat in the middle of the temple, next to the central tree where Parlòp sat. It mewled confusedly to itself and stared dourly at the stranger.

He pulled himself out of the water and up onto the nearest of the trees that formed the base of the temple. He stopped some twenty feet from her. The water was cascading off his sodden robe but he didn't even look down at it. The stranger bowed a greeting to her. Then he leaned against the trunk of a tree, but he did not speak.

Parlòp sat and considered him in silence for a long while. There was a belt around his waist. Many objects were hanging from it. Parlòp recognised very few of them. Still, the stranger did not speak. He moved slowly up and perched on the tree where he was and looked back at her. There was nothing in his gaze that usually filled the gaze of men when they looked at Parlòp's naked green-hued body. He waited for her to assess him.

'And who are you?' she said eventually.

'I am just a stranger passing through,' he said. 'I have come for the crystal. It is not meant for this age. We did not know it was still there, in the laboratories of Vyderbo. We should not have left it for people to find. Then all that has happened would ... could have been avoided. But the anger and ambition of people would not have changed and they would have found another reason to vie with each other and to fight. People would still die. There is always hatred and ambition. It is too often so.'

'What makes you think I have it? It was destroyed ... Caresma ...' She had spent hours telling her Grandee and the Solpsari the same things. It had been destroyed. She repeated all the words, presented her story. He did not interrupt or contradict her. She stopped. He did not respond. Parlòp gazed at him.

Then the stranger nodded sagely as if considering her words but she knew that he understood they were untrue. He spoke. 'Caresma, his real name was Poxuul, I think, did not destroy it as he wished. Nor did he carry it away with him. He was subsumed by it. He was, as you know, one of the makkuz, a watcher. He was disguised as a man but he was not one. The crystal took him into itself. He was constructed of energy as all the thybuk and shadii are. The crystal can store or draw all types of energeia to itself. He was depleted by it. He perished.' He looked across at her, his countenance calm and unhurried. 'And you carried it away, to hide it from the gaze of the ambitious and the violent – to keep it safe. To preserve our world.'

She did not deny it but turned and looked across at the shadow beast. He had stopped mewling by her tree and was gazing at them both with strange, quizzical eyes. Parlòp voiced the shadow beast to be calm for all was well. She hoped it was. She turned back and looked beyond the stranger to the jaksar sitting waiting patiently on the far bank. Nothing flowed from the forest creature's understanding except absolute trust in his companion, this stranger who sat silently opposite her.

'Such a device should not exist in the world,' she said. 'To create our dreams and nightmares is not a skill that people should have.' She considered him. 'Why should I give it to you any more than all those others.' She paused. 'Even if I possessed it.'

The stranger nodded. 'Such power should not exist. Or should not be used in such a way. Such an ability is too great, too much for those who crave power and dominance. But Parlòp, it was not made for the task to which it was put. It was not constructed for that reason. Kalanomena, and those others, turned it, used it that way. It is merely a conduit, a locus, a way of garnering energeia. More precisely it channels energy from the universe. Kalanomena used the enormous energy it can furnish to give solidity to his dreams of power and dominance. He used that ability to construct nightmares.'

Parlòp considered this. 'So what then is it for? If it is not a maker crystal?'

The stranger shook his head. 'It isn't a maker. It merely pulls energeia into itself. And the energy it channels is not as you might understand it, not as anyone there in the vault of Vyderbo understood.' The stranger picked up a clod of dirt and, holding it, looked at it carefully. 'There are five forces in the world, in the universe, mystic Parlòp.' He held the soil up as if it was for a moment the whole universe. 'Five essences some have called them. There is the energeia that gives us light and heat, an essence that gives us life and illumination. The second essence keeps us upon this ground and stops all the world from flying off into chaotic nothingness. It attracts, it balances and it holds. It is active over huge distances. It is how the world and the sun dance together. There are two other essences which operate in the realm of the very small.' He picked a tiny leaf from the tree branch he was sitting on and held it up next to the clod. 'Not this smallness, but the infinitesimal that makes this earth up, indeed it makes everything up. One of these two essences is very strong and the other is very weak. Between them, they mould the world. But there is a fifth essence that opposes the others. It pushes apart instead of gathering together. There is a great deal of this fifth essence in the universe. Some think it a dark energeia.' He stopped talking and gazed across at her. His look was not the look of someone trying to decide if she understood but the look of a person waiting as she absorbed and appreciated his words.

'The crystal,' he went on, 'was tuned to gather this fifth essence, to draw upon it. This is why Kalanomena was able to create matter itself because he took the essence, the dark energeia that the crystal draws from the universe and he used it for his dream of creation.' The stranger looked, for a moment, profoundly sad. 'But this is true of most wisdom found in the world. What comes first is the thought, the cleverness, the piece of wisdom. But how people choose to use the cleverness, what we do with it, is the final quandary. How we use the powers the world gives us – that is a decision we make. Your people protect the knowledge of the way of the beast – because you know otherwise it will be misused. You are right. So it is with the crystal.'

'So, if I had it to give to you . . . what would you do with it?'

'It would disappear. It would be used no longer by people hungry for power like ravening hakkat.' He looked up. 'We store energy for the future times. It would merely be secured for the time when the Malasar, the magician kings of old, return.'

Parlòp shook her head. 'And why would they use it for the right purpose? Would they not turn this thing against the people, against peace, just as everyone has done?'

He smiled a strangely direct smile and then shrugged. 'You are right to be suspicious. I can do no more than speak the words. You must trust me, or you must not.' He stared across at her. 'But, mystic Parlòp, hear me. The hostile ravening ones will learn that you live, that you did not die on Vyderbo with all the others. Then they will begin to wonder whether, as you survived, you did not leave with the powerful relic they crave. They will not know, but their suspicion will be enough. You will be sought out. And even if you successfully disguise the truth from them, what will happen to the crystal when you die? Who will finally protect it? Will they not tear the swamp apart to find it?'

She did not respond. Would her tree protect it enough? Would the river take it to the deep ocean to be lost there? Or would the savage hakkat come and burn her tree?

The stranger sighed. 'If you give it to me, I will place it in the hands of Franeus himself, the one true maven, the everlasting priest. He has bound himself to the Everlasting Caves until Arnex awakes. He alone knows how this thing must be used and what dangers it poses. He will protect it for all time. You cannot.'

Parlòp considered this stranger. 'It was Franeus himself who taught us the way of the beasts, taught us the Voice, the Summoning, the Understanding and the Order. He is truly in the Caves then? He still lives?'

The stranger nodded. 'He always is. He is everlasting. He would have come to you himself, mystic Parlòp, but he cannot . . . will not leave the Caves until he is released from his oath. Only when the Right Hand his brother returns will he come. Yet he awaits your decision here, mystic Parlòp. He knows I have come before you. We will not coerce you. The choice is yours. You may keep this thing.' He raised his head. 'But you should not.'

The jaksar still sitting waiting on the far riverbank yowled. Parlòp looked round at the beast. He had voiced her! The beasts give understanding. They cannot voice. What jaksar was this?

She looked back at the stranger. 'The jaksar tells me to trust you.'

'Insnar and I have travelled together for a long while. He stands with me too and waits as I do when I am not required.' The stranger smiled his peculiar, open smile. 'But you must decide, Parlòp. It was your role to save the world from this thing.'

She rose to her feet. 'That is all I have ever sought,' she said, 'from the very first moment I understood.'

The stranger did not move. 'And is it your role to keep it? To hide from the predatory?'

Parlòp touched the bark of the central tree on which she sat and let herself drink in the calm of its vegetation, its plantness, its utter and secure safeness. The tree knew it was valued. It knew she wished only its good. The bark before her hand opened and she reached in and pulled the crystal from its depths. She held it up to the light and stared at the strange energeia swirling deep inside it. She turned and looked at the stranger. He had not moved. He was not going to come in violence to seize the crystal from her.

'What of the beast?' She turned and looked at the shadow beast sitting next to her, lost in fear but not distraught enough to flee from this stranger and his jaksar companion. It trusted them, as much as it ever could.

The stranger smiled again. 'It did not ask for life. Yet it deserves its existence. It is. It should have all that any of us have.' He looked piercingly at Parlòp. 'You care. Keep it as your companion as Insnar is mine. When the ravening hakkat come to take the crystal from you, it will give them pause. It will fight for you. It cares for you as you care for it. So walk with it. It will not live longer than any beast and you can make its life worth the living. You can assuage its fear at the last, and give it peace.'

Parlòp looked at the stranger and then the beast. 'I am afraid for it. It does not eat. Cannot eat, it appears. It does not understand food. It will not live long without some means of sustenance. I do not know how it has lived this long.'

The stranger shook his head. 'It was born of the shadow energeia and a man's tortured mind. It is made of his broken ambition and hatred. It feeds now on the same hidden fifth essence, the dark energeia of which it is constructed. It will live. It will not perish before its proper time.'

Parlòp walked over to the stranger. He rose slowly to his feet and waited for her. She held the crystal out and dropped it into his waiting hands.

'Do not destroy this world, stranger,' she said.

'No, I will not,' he said. 'It will be restored. But not yet . . . Arnex must awake.'

'So be it,' she said. She knew the myths. Perhaps they were true.

She returned to the tree that had kept the gem for her. She stroked it gently and then took her staff from the branch. She held it close to her body. The shadow beast looked at her questioningly.

She stretched it out and offered it to the stranger.

'Keep that,' he said. 'I have recovered the other. It is yours. I know you will use it wisely. And one day, give it to someone worthy of the name of mystic. And when you finally join with the swamp of your birth, it will be fully theirs.'

The stranger slipped the crystal into a pouch at his belt and then he left her. He did not look back. She went and took the shadow beast into her arms. An odd feeling swept through her – the feeling of a job completed, a thing well done, the pride in beauty created.

As the stranger and his jaksar went their way, she thought she could hear him singing.

Lightning Source UK Ltd.
Milton Keynes UK
UKHW021310021122
411515UK00025B/878